SPECIAL MESSAGE

THE ULVERSCROFT FOUNDATION

(registered UK charity number 264873)

was established in 1972 to provide funds for research, diagnosis and treatment of eye diseases.
Examples of major projects funded by the Ulverscroft Foundation are:-

- The Children's Eye Unit at Moorfields Eye Hospital, London
- The Ulverscroft Children's Eye Unit at Great Ormond Street Hospital for Sick Children
- Funding research into eye diseases and treatment at the Department of Ophthalmology, University of Leicester
- The Ulverscroft Vision Research Group, Institute of Child Health
- Twin operating theatres at the Western Ophthalmic Hospital, London
- The Chair of Ophthalmology at the Royal Australian College of Ophthalmologists

You can help further the work of the Foundation by making a donation or leaving a legacy. Every contribution is gratefully received. If you would like to help support the Foundation or require further information, please contact:

THE ULVERSCROFT FOUNDATION
The Green, Bradgate Road, Anstey
Leicester LE7 7FU, England
Tel: (0116) 236 4325

website: www.foundation.ulverscroft.com

Noelene Jenkinson has lived all her life in the heartland of the Victorian Wimmera wheatbelt in Australia. She is married with two daughters and five grandchildren, and lives with her husband on 1.5 acres in a passive solar home surrounded by a native garden. Besides writing and reading, she also loves Australian history, card-making, playing her electronic keyboard, crocheting afghan rugs, and genealogy.

EMMA'S PLACE

Thirty-something jeweller Emma Hamilton returns to her childhood hometown of Tingara, a charming historic village in the foothills of the Australian Alps. Builder Malcolm Webster commutes to Tingara from nearby Bendigo each weekend to work on restoring a beautiful old Victorian homestead. When the two meet, attraction flares — but Mal is young; and Emma, wary after her failed marriage, is not in the market for romance. Will Mal's humour and charm break down her barriers?

Books by Noelene Jenkinson
Published by Ulverscroft:

A WHIRLWIND ROMANCE
OUTBACK HERO
STARTING AGAIN
OCEAN BLUE
NANNY WANTED
WOMBAT CREEK
GRACE'S COTTAGE
A GENTLEMAN'S BRIDE
WHISPERS ON THE PLAINS
BENEATH AN OUTBACK SKY

NOELENE JENKINSON

EMMA'S PLACE

Complete and Unabridged

ULVERSCROFT
Leicester

First published in Great Britain in 2016

First Large Print Edition
published 2017

The moral right of the author has been asserted

A catalogue record for this book is available
from the British Library.

ISBN 978–1–4448–3262–4

Published by
F. A. Thorpe (Publishing)
Anstey, Leicestershire

Set by Words & Graphics Ltd.
Anstey, Leicestershire
Printed and bound in Great Britain by
T. J. International Ltd., Padstow, Cornwall

This book is printed on acid-free paper

1

Emma's striding footsteps pounded the quiet early morning streets of Tingara, cushioned by thick layers of autumn leaves littering the ground. The early morning fog had thinned but the crisp frosty air nipped her bare ears and face.

Trotting ahead, Gran's dog, Mate, yanked on his leash, eager to escape. She should release him to scamper off and live dangerously in the woodland bordering the sheltered path. Snuffle and hunt for nothing much in the bush. But this morning's fierce biting air persuaded her to head back for Gran's cosy flat.

With her free hand she tugged her beanie lower and her scarf tighter.

Accustomed to Sydney's milder climate for years, Emma had forgotten Tingara's numbing cold. Nestled in northern Victoria near the foothills of the mountains that formed a spine along the east coast, it was only a one hour drive to the snowfields.

She had loved growing up here and been devastated to leave when her family moved away.

But now Emma had returned, arriving last year, seeking sanctuary, time and space to reshuffle her thoughts and life. As she walked, smoke trailed from chimneys as fires were lit or stoked into life again. She inhaled deeply of their woodsy smells.

Leaving the bush track she turned into Wattle Gully Road back toward the village that had become her home. Without question, Gran had graciously welcomed her smarting granddaughter.

Emma slowed as she passed the grand old Victorian weatherboard Webster place, *Clovelly*. Lights blazed in every window, its double panelled front door wide open even on this chilly morning. Odd. She often came this way on her morning jaunts when Mate took her for a walk before breakfast. The place was usually quiet and deserted but was alive with action on this particular Saturday, a white twin cab ute like a tradesman's vehicle backed into the driveway, its tailgate down, presumably for unloading.

She boldly dawdled and stared inside as she passed. A young bloke with dark curly hair was working halfway up a ladder. From her brief teasing glimpse he appeared handsome in a boyish way. Not too bad looking actually, if you liked them younger. She certainly wasn't looking. She was still a married woman. Which, much to her annoyance, reminded her she really needed to do something about that.

On those thoughts and at that exact moment her mobile rang, sounding twice as loud when it echoed in the stillness. As she grabbed for it, the man glanced sharply out the window in her direction, catching her gaping. Awkward. A jolt of alarm flared between them like the look of a wild animal caught in headlights.

Trapped, Emma smiled weakly and waved then turned her back. 'Hello, this is Emma Hamilton.'

She used her maiden name these days and cringed as her voice echoed forever above the silence. Deciding it was best to leave, not look back and keep talking as she walked in case the young dreamboat was still staring, Emma moved on.

'Hey Emma. It's Stacey.'

The bubbly half of a newly engaged young local couple who had commissioned Emma to design and make their ring gushed on the other end of the phone.

'It's ready for you.' Emma knew a brief tweak of envy even as she tried to sound upbeat and happy for them. After a squeal of delight from the other end, she added, 'I'll be in my studio at The Stables by ten, okay?'

'Perfect. We'll see you then.'

Stacey sounded like an excited teenager and Emma guessed she wasn't much older. Ah, young love! She sighed, jamming the phone back into her coat pocket and taking a short cut across the town park by the rotunda with its elaborate timber arches and exposed rafters beneath the domed roof.

Sniffing his closeness to home and a warm doggie bed inside Gran's back porch, Mate led the way at a run. Emma jogged to keep up. The Bakery Cafe had been open since six. The fresh sweet smell of bread and sticky buns mixed with the heavenly aroma of freshly roasted coffee wafting from inside sent her stomach rumbling. The cafe opened daily and weekends were the goldmine for every business in this tourist region all year. Which had also proven lucrative for Emma's work

As they approached it, she admired Gran's neat red brick flat and cottage garden although the roses were bare and needed a prune. Somehow her green fingered grand-mother kept it colourful all year.

Emma unleashed Mate in the porch and he immediately scampered inside to find his mistress. Mate was Gran's beloved little companion rescued from an animal shelter soon after grandpa Henry died. Emma hung up her coat.

As she entered the compact kitchen, Gran turned and smiled. 'Kettle's boiled.'

Toast cooled in a rack and Mary Hamilton, still in her cosy blue dressing gown sat at the round table in the breakfast alcove halfway through a bowl of porridge.

'Morning Gran.' Emma kissed the top of her head. She poured a coffee and sat opposite. 'Someone's renovating the Webster place.'

'So I hear.'

'And?' Emma prompted. Living a hectic social life in Tingara all her life, Gran knew everything and everyone so she was sure to have the answer.

'We all wondered what would happen to that dear old property after crusty old George died last year. It's been empty ever since. Happened just before you arrived, dear. I can tell you, few people wanted to be at *that* funeral. They only attended out of respect. Logical the boys want to sell. No love lost between them and their father.'

'How do you know it's up for sale?'

'Auction notice went up in Anne Kelly's real estate agent window yesterday.'

Emma grinned to herself. Whereas she hadn't noticed, Gran and every other nosy or elderly local missed nothing in town. Given a choice, that lovely old Victorian, *Clovelly*, even in its faded grandeur, would be close to her own vision of a dream family home.

Except she didn't have a family and was gripped by a brief fit of the doldrums. As much as she loved her younger sister Julie's pre-schoolers, Zach and Mia, Emma sometimes filled with envy. She couldn't watch all that cuteness and joy in other families and still remain detached and unaffected. She craved it for herself.

Meanwhile Gran had continued talking over her thoughts.

'Families don't always turn out the way we'd like. The Websters were always flawed. George's fault. Tough cranky old codger. And take my dear son, Clive, that useless father of yours, too,' Mary muttered.

Emma reflected. Hard to picture easy going Clive as the son of such a busy and dynamic woman like her grandmother.

'He slipped through the cracks of my discipline. I take some responsibility for that. His own nature and attitude must bear the rest. Disappointing.' She shook her head. 'I'm sorry he wasn't the best role model for you.'

'Not your fault, Gran. Dad's a dreamer, not a doer. He tries hard and means well, and he's devoted to Mum.'

'It's admirable that Alice stuck with him all these years but she always was gullible.'

6

One endeavour or business after another of her father's ventures had failed because Clive Hamilton never stuck to one long enough to see it through. Sadly, this meant their man of the house as provider tended to be unreliable. All of which set the family on the path of insecurity and kept money tight as Emma, Richard and Julie grew up. Even though she didn't look it, their mother Alice was the strong one, always making excuses for her husband. She was the support beam that held everything together in their family.

'On the other hand, Dad's so hopeless and lovable, I can understand why Mum fell in love with him. And still does.'

'Love *is* blind,' Gran said with conviction.

Emma cringed and felt inadequate. She wouldn't know. Steve had been charming, too. She had fallen quickly and deeply under his spell. But within three years her marriage, to whom she believed at the time was her dream man, had gradually fallen apart. Great gaps appeared in their differences. They argued about lifestyle, priorities and other subjects never raised or discussed up front. And then there had always been the other women. Emma had failed miserably at her choice of partner and her own attempt at the family she always wanted.

Children and a proper home, not a cold

cube of an apartment in Darling Point, even if it did overlook fabulous waterside views with its iconic opera house and arched harbour bridge.

Mary finished breakfast and shuffled over to the sink to wash the dishes. 'You'll be in The Stables all weekend again, I suppose?' she murmured wryly.

Emma cleared and wiped the table and grabbed a tea towel, backed up against the counter while Gran ran sudsy water. She knew Gran despaired of her non-existent social life and nodded. 'Stacey and Joey are coming to collect their ring at ten. Cold weather eases tourist numbers but my sales are steady enough no matter what the season.'

'You shouldn't bury yourself in your work. Leave that studio of yours sometimes. Get out and socialise. Go clubbing.'

'In Tingara!' Emma chuckled. 'There isn't one. Besides, I can't afford to close up and lose potential business.' A hollow protest, and she knew it, suspecting the direction this conversation was drifting. 'Weekends are the busiest time in town. You know that. Besides, I love making jewellery and I have to earn a living.'

'Phooey.' Gran rejected her excuses. 'You said you have enough to live on for now. Give

8

yourself a break. Go down to the pub. Attractive thing like you should be having a good time.'

'I'm a second hand woman,' she grumbled. 'I failed last time. Not sure I should try again.'

'Never took you for a coward. Besides, you're not so special. Half the marriages today end in divorce.'

Emma grew thoughtful and glanced out the window as she wiped cutlery and put them in the drawer. 'Why do you think that is, Gran?' she asked quietly.

If she wanted to move on, she could do with some honest advice. And if there was one person who was up front and who would tell her like it is, not sugar coated to save her feelings, it was her grandmother.

'I'm not sure present generations are prepared to persevere for life like we did, dear. Probably sensible. Many of our generation stayed in unhappy marriages out of habit or security. We often didn't work outside the home and raised our family while the man worked so we depended on them. They were different social times with different expectations. That didn't mean we were content. We just accepted our lot and endured, I think.'

'But you and Grandpa were happy?'

Mary smiled softly. 'Oh, yes, dear. Henry was so polite and thoughtful.' Her gaze drifted out the window. 'We loved and respected each other every day of our lives.'

'I adored Steve.'

'Notice you spoke in the past tense, dear. True love may fade after the first intensity and glow but if it's real and has the indefinable *something*, it lasts. It's always there in the background.' She cast her granddaughter a side glance. 'You must know why it didn't work between you and Steve, dear?'

This was one of the few times Gran had raised the subject of Emma's separation. She had skirted around the edges a few times, sent out hints, that sort of thing, but never directly probed, like now.

Should Emma disillusion her grandmother and tell her the truth? On the brink of disclosure, Emma scuttled away from it at the last second before opening her mouth.

'Because I was blind with passion and adoration for him and fell like a sinker. If anyone had tried to talk me out of marrying him at the time, I wouldn't have listened.'

Emma's father had been unmotivated. Steve was ambitious. Had she subconsciously chosen her husband for the wrong reasons? True. She *had* been smitten. She didn't see past the suit and nice car, high paying job and happiness she was sure would always survive. Chose to ignore her partner's lingering looks over other females even before they were engaged. Tolerated them even after marriage, believed his excuses and accepted the gifts when she still remained unsure and forgiving.

Ultimately, Emma no longer knew respect and loyalty from Steve. He had laughed off and brushed aside her concerns, telling her to chill and live for today. On that sour note, she had known their marriage could not survive.

'Steve wasn't for you, dear.'

Gran's words invaded Emma's thoughts and she sighed. 'No.'

'He was too flash. A city boy. You're a small town girl at heart.'

'How do you work that one out?' Emma said indignantly knowing, with thanks to Steve and his high profile contacts, she had risen to the top of her game in her jewellery business in Sydney with an income to prove it.

'You came straight back here to Tingara without a second thought when you needed to, didn't you?'

Emma couldn't argue with that. Licking wounds equalled Tingara.

Gran said, 'I'm guessing the significance of today hasn't escaped you?'

Of course it hadn't. Out walking Mate earlier, Emma had reflected on the relevance of this day on the calendar in her life. On what she wanted as she moved forward.

A family. Simple as that. Her parents were contentedly married. They had personality contrasts certainly, which in their case proved complimentary but they were still devoted to each other. For them it was all about respect, compromise and understanding. Clive and Alice Hamilton were still in love after decades of marriage. Nothing special for some. They clicked and were just meant to be together.

Observing them over the years, it wasn't a connection they could teach. It was almost as if her parents were silently communicating *watch and learn, children*, without actually saying a word. Emma's only regret in their family life had been their parents' lack of engagement with their own children. Leaving them as adults realising they had been short changed.

Emma knew now she wanted that kind of lifetime relationship for herself even though her father had always been less than useless. Was it even sensible these days to dream of lasting love? Her younger sister Julie was happily married, so far, after almost six years, to Chris with her nephew and niece, Zach and Mia. Their older brother, Richard, of course still unattached and surfing.

Looking back on her own relationship, meeting Steve had been like a blast of warm air. She became caught up in its swirling vortex. He'd been fun, strong and influential. Caught up in his glitzy fast-paced life, Emma had been carried along in his exciting wake. Her parents had been impressed. Steve was the ambitious achiever, the complete opposite of her father.

Her mother's lips had quivered and her eyes glistened with the makings of tears, the day she told her parents she was leaving Steve. She hadn't gone into detail, merely said it wasn't working for them and their lives were heading along different paths. All very surface at the time but it had been enough.

Emma had then told Alice and Clive that Gran had agreed to let her go and live with her.

Her mother hadn't faked surprise. 'Back to Tingara where you were born? Are you sure, dear? You've been in the city half your life now. You might find it dull returning to a small country town,' she warned gently.

Emma swiftly reassured her. If her mother knew how unhappy and bored she had become in the last two years enduring Steve's infidelity, Alice Hamilton might not have so readily questioned her daughter's choice.

She had deliberately not told her parents the truth about her husband and burst the idealised image they had of their son-in-law. The success, wealth and high social circles in which he moved which, by default, included their daughter, brought bragging rights into their prosaic suburban life.

Emma had decided to let them hold onto their false dreams a while longer. Until they'd had time to adjust to her new single status in life apart from Steve. Then she would seek the inevitable divorce.

So far Steve had not made the first move either. Emma wasn't surprised. He was probably too busy making money and philandering. Although that tag was not strictly correct any longer since they were officially separated. He could do as he pleased now. Emma had neither asked nor expected anything from him when she left. She had only sought her freedom. A complete break from all she had known in Sydney all those years.

And she had certainly found it in quaint and unassuming Tingara, her childhood home. Emma discovered she loved it again now as much as she had years ago. Thrived here, in fact. She had established a new life and business career with Gran happily encouraging her to stay as long as she needed.

But with the passing of a year, Emma wondered if security was such a good thing. She was aware that decisions needed to be made. She just hadn't found the push to action yet.

Eventually, Emma sighed, pulling herself back to reality and the present moment. 'Today is the first anniversary of the day I left Steve of course.'

'And that means . . . ?'

'We've been legally separated for a year and after one more day I can apply for a divorce.'

'Good girl. It's called the future, dear. Grab it.'

'No pressure!' Emma scoffed. 'It's daunting to think of starting again,' she admitted. 'Putting myself out there. Dating. Yuck.'

In her heart she wanted a divorce and knew there was no option for any other course. It wasn't that she didn't want to be married again. It was the logical option for creating that family she fantasised about. She just no longer wanted to be married to Steve.

Which raised the question bugging her all year. Where to next? Where to settle? With no ties, she could live anywhere in the world she chose. Emma realised she would be perfectly happy living somewhere like Tingara where she had grown up. It was familiar, comfortable. Or should she stretch her boundaries and move someplace completely new?

'There's so much competition out there,' Emma moaned. 'Older men are looking for younger women. Available men over thirty are scarce as dinosaurs.'

'Then lower your age limit.' Mary tossed her granddaughter a knowing *look*.

Emma was stunned by her statement and her thoughts flashed to the young stud on the ladder in *Clovelly*. No. She was ticking along just fine thank you. She had peace. She didn't need another man in her life. She had hooked up too fast with Steve and look how that ended. She wouldn't repeat that mistake. Like *ever*.

⋆ ⋆ ⋆

The Stables at the end of Tingara's main street was a big old restored and rustic two storey brick barn of a building loaded with historical features and atmosphere. A town landmark. Crafts people and artisans occupied stalls around the perimeter or spaces beneath the windows on both lower and loft levels. All accessed by a new purpose built wide central staircase.

By the time Emma arrived, other traders

had already opened up and organised their wares. She waved, smiled or greeted her nearest neighbours as she passed.

In her own workshop and well lit showcase display, she prepared for Stacey and Joey's appointment and, in the light of her own life mess, pretended to be happy for the youthful pair. Within minutes of her arrival and opening, they appeared, beaming with expectation.

Emma welcomed them and offered a seat. Then produced her assigned masterpiece and lifted the lid. Nestled amid plush black velvet, the ring's diamond and gold setting gleamed beneath the natural light.

With sighs and gasps from Stacey, Emma gestured for Joey to slip it on his fiancée's finger for a final fitting. Making Emma all the more aware of her own bare hands, devoid of her own wedding jewellery, promptly removed, to remain hidden in their exclusive jeweller's boxes before leaving Sydney.

Stacey's eyes glittered with tears. A gaze of such adoring happiness and glowing love passed between the smitten twosome as they looked into each other's eyes. Emma tactfully rose and withdrew to allow them a moment of privacy on this special moment in their lives.

All couples started out with such blind love. Why couldn't they always get it to work? Emma stopped short of screaming out *Has it all been just about sex for you two? Or have you even considered sitting down together and really talking to each other about your expectations of your union and future dreams?*

Emma hardened herself against such mushy idolatry. Yuck. It was pathetic. Just as she had been. Once. Who needed it? Marriage was unpredictable. Things happened. Life changed. She mentally shook her head. Not going there again.

Then she felt bad for thinking ill of the marital fate for these dreamy youngsters, consigning them to doom before they had barely started.

Stacey and Joey gushed their thanks, more importantly paid for Emma's creation then left, radiant and holding hands.

* * *

Business continued briskly in The Stables all day with Emma's signature chandelier necklace and earring combinations always popular.

Sunday morning, Mate pulled Emma along again on their familiar early morning walk.

Later than usual. Difficult to cast aside a snug doona these days to squander a few more minutes of lazy time. Her new simple life was reason enough to get up each day. She loved her creative work. Besides, Gran appreciated someone else walking Mate. Her octogenarian grandmother had always been an active lady but couldn't walk as fast or as far as she would like these days.

The stunning autumn colours made up for the post dawn start though. In weeks, branches would be bare but for now, the village landscape was all eye catching orange, gold and showy reds.

The bakery and cafes already hummed with breakfast tourist custom, their lights blazing a warm welcoming glow out onto the sombre early morning street. Enticing coffee smells drifted into the senses while the weak sun tried to push its way through the usual misty veil of fog that hushed everything.

Feeling snoopy as Mate strained ahead and she headed down Wattle Gully Road on the edge of town, Emma deliberately strode past *Clovelly* again. The vehicle was gone and the house silent. Bursting with curiosity despite knowing she was trespassing, Emma crept up the front path and cupped her hands against one of the front bay windows under the veranda to peer inside. The rooms were virtually unfurnished except for a lounge chair, small table and a mattress. Surely squatters hadn't moved in already?

'Can I help you?'

Emma let out a screech and whirled around, a hand on her chest over her thumping heart. The young man stood halfway along the path. Caught out, she squirmed with guilt.

'Didn't see anyone around,' she flustered, feeling hot.

At closer range today, the face above the bags of groceries he carried was gorgeous, the dark curly hair, longish and brushing the shoulders of his hooded parka, abundant and deeply appealing. But he was far too young to be given a second glance by an older woman. She sighed. Bet he turned young girls' heads though.

'There's usually no one here except me on weekends,' he explained, unsmiling, but a glint of devilry sparkled deep behind the eyes that swept over her from the beanie to her hiker boots. Really, could she look any more rustic in her trackies and knitted hat from the op shop Gran had convinced her to buy?

She looked over his shoulder toward the road. 'No vehicle today?' He must have walked into town.

'It's parked out back for security at night.'

Tricked on that one, then. 'You're fairly safe in Tingara. All the same,' she waved an arm in the air, 'Sorry to intrude.'

'No you're not,' he teased and shrugged. 'I'll bet most locals are interested in what's happening to this place. Natural to be curious. Been unoccupied all year. It's not my house.' He glanced up and over it with obvious admiration. 'I'm just working on the renovations.'

'You know the owners then?'

He seemed amused by her suggestion. 'Yes. You a local?'

Was she? 'Yes and no. Just staying in town for a while.' If you considered one year temporary.

She dared not reveal she lived with her grandmother. How lame would that sound to a young stud like this? She could imagine the headline. *Woman pushing middle age lives with granny.* Which didn't really reflect her life's experiences.

He strode up the steps and joined her under the veranda. Up close and staring into them, his eyes were misty watercolour blue, dreamy and absorbing. Just as hers were as dark as the russet leaves falling all over the place right now.

She cleared her throat and played the older responsible adult in control. 'Emma.' She extended her hand and he shook it warmly, wrapping his big rough hand around hers.

'Mal. I've noticed you out and about in the mornings.'

He had used the plural *mornings*. Emma was taken back by his personal observation. Then remembered the phone call yesterday when he heard and saw her passing. She frowned. The cheeky glance he shot at her left hand said *No rings and available*. Was he flirting? She felt alarmed and flattered. Not to mention annoyed that with all her experience of them, she didn't immediately recognise another womaniser.

'I guess this is a big job,' she rambled on, looking back through a window to break his gaze and cover her discomfort.

'Yep.' He nodded and tossed a bunch of keys.

'Going to take some time then.'

'A few months but it's a grand old home and worth it. Needs to be done properly.' His enthusiasm started to leak out. 'Fortunately all the original features are still intact. The ceiling roses, the carved timber mantels and old fireplaces. All working.'

Emma could have lingered but began to feel foolish chatting with this Generation Y heartbreaker.

'Well, good luck.' She edged toward the

steps and departure, tugging Mate to follow.

'See you around,' he said over his shoulder as he juggled his grocery bags and unlocked the front door. 'Unless you have time to come in for a sneak peek,' he called out.

Emma froze. She could hardly believe her ears. Who would pass up that invitation? She shouldn't. Gossip for Gran, she reasoned?

'Oh. Really?' She didn't want to sound too eager. 'Your time must be tight if you only have weekends.'

He grinned and stepped aside, gesturing for her to enter. 'Be my guest. Bring your dog,' he coaxed when she deliberately hesitated. 'This is a work site at the moment. Muddy paws won't matter.'

'Mate is house trained.' Emma didn't hesitate. She wiped her feet and entered, unclipping Mate's leash. 'Everyone in town is gossiping about what's happening here.'

'I figured.' Mal went on ahead and dumped his groceries on a carpenter's work bench in the kitchen. She followed. Mate promptly disappeared.

Mal planted his hands on his hips. 'This is still a shell, as you can see. I'm building custom made cupboards in my Bendigo workshop. Kind of French provincial look to modernise it but still with a traditional country feel.'

Emma nodded. So, he lived a few hours away.

'Planning all new fittings in the bathrooms, too,' he continued, 'But basically I'm just repairing any structural work that needs it and updating, then I'll give the whole house a fresh lick of paint inside and out and I'm done.'

'Impressive. My kind of place.'

'Yeah. Mine, too.' He glanced about longingly. 'But I can't afford a grand old place like this. Garden's going to need a complete makeover as well. The bones of its original layout are there. Be best to restore it in the same era it was built.'

'For sure. Needs an old fashioned flower garden. Border beds. Rows of lavender. Lattice arch smothered with a climbing rose.' Emma shrugged, seeing it all clearly in her mind. 'Herb parterre maybe?'

'Be easy enough to replicate. Just need to find a landscaper.'

'My Gran lives in town. She's a keen gardener. She's bound to know someone.'

'Would you mind asking?'

Emma shook her head. 'Not at all.' A sneaky little voice in her head said *So now you have an excuse to see him again, don't you?*

Mal led her through the rest of the large

rambling house with generous rooms, high ceilings and sash windows. They wandered back through the front grand and spacious reception rooms featuring the bay windows one saw from the road.

Reluctantly, Emma whistled for Mate. He trotted obediently to her side and she clipped on his lead again.

'Thanks for the tour.'

'So, where do I find you?' Mal asked with a cheeky grin.

Emma laughed and waved. He was great for morale. 'Tingara's small enough. I'll be around.'

She just knew he would be watching her as she left. She didn't know if that was a good or a bad thing but she had no intention of turning around. All the same, Mal whoever-he-was was good for the soul. Attractive for sure, friendly if flirty but otherwise uncomplicated. She needed to keep it that way.

After that, Emma couldn't wait to get back to Gran's flat. As she walked in the back door, Mate went straight to his mistress for an affectionate pat.

'You were a while this morning.'

'Only made it to this end of Wattle Gully Road. *Clovelly* actually. I met the builder who's renovating the place. Mal someone.' Emma flickered her eyebrows. 'He showed me through. It's gorgeous.'

'Mal? Short for Malcolm maybe?' The name seemed to spark the older woman's interest and memory and she frowned. 'Now why does that name sound familiar?' She shook her head. 'It will come to me I expect.'

'He needs a gardener for a makeover before the auction. Know anyone in town for such a big job?'

Gran sighed. 'Only Ivy our florist. She's getting too old but she certainly has the experience and would be loaded with ideas. And she used to have a connection with the place. I'll ask.'

★ ★ ★

Emma found herself restless and the following weekdays dragged. Monday she had pointlessly walked past *Clovelly* but all was quiet. What else did she expect? So she chose new and alternate paths around the town's central park, and along Stony Creek to distance her thoughts from a certain handsome young man who had set her heart racing but was, thinking sensibly, out of bounds. Why? Because of his age and, besides, she wasn't looking. Hadn't been all year and didn't intend to start now.

She hardly saw anything of Gran all week,

who busily volunteered at the local historical society, was regularly rostered on at the op shop, besides her cards and bingo afternoons. Probably a good thing. At least they didn't get under each other's feet and Gran always returned in the evenings chatty and brimming with the day's news.

Wednesday, she ran into Will Bennett, about the only one of her old school friends still in town. He had been the untidiest kid in class and least likely to succeed at anything. His ambitious professional parents had despaired.

Because the aromas drew them in and neither had any commitments nor was in a hurry, and because conversation with Will was always easy and uncomplicated, Emma accepted his invitation to coffee in the Bakery Cafe. The two former schoolies simply enjoyed each other's company and often found themselves reminiscing which usually demanded a second cup of coffee.

Over countless previous brews this past year both in the cafe and Will's unconventional home, Emma learnt he was now a talented and successful artist. Although on leaving school, he had decided not to completely disappoint his family and studied architecture. But not before he had done the beach bum thing like her brother Richard, gathered his thoughts together and grew up a bit.

Emma often wondered if Will might have a thing happening with the city business executive, Ginny Bates, who lived a few doors down from Will in Gum Tree Lane. She had bought the former St. Anne's chapel as a weekender of sorts. Will had been instrumental in helping redesign and convert the building into a home. Because they spent time together, rumours circulated about the pair but Ginny only visited Tingara on occasional weekends and Will hardly seemed smitten. He never mentioned her.

Besides, the pair seemed an unlikely match. Will was as casual and anti-establishment as Ginny was high powered and meticulous. These days, Will's casual mismatched dress and long hair could only be termed *alternative*. If he and Ginny were an item, she would have him in chinos and a polo shirt with a sweater casually draped around his shoulders. Emma mentally tried to conjure up the image and shook her head. No. Couldn't see it. Ginny wasn't Will's type at all.

As off-handedly as possible, Emma mentioned Mal renovating *Clovelly* but Will already knew. So she moved on to confide in him about her brewing divorce.

'Why haven't *you* ever married?' she asked him bluntly.

'So far no one wants me.' He grinned, outwardly unperturbed.

'Their loss. You're a decent catch. But not for me though.' She laid a hand gently on his arm when he flickered his eyebrows hopefully. 'Two artists under one roof? Recipe for disaster. We'd drive each other nuts.'

'Or complement each other,' he teased.

'If there was any spark we'd have felt it by now,' Emma chuckled.

When Emma told Gran of the meeting that evening when both returned to the flat, she hinted, 'He's your age and not married. What's holding you back?'

Emma scoffed. 'No chemistry. We don't have that . . . connection. Will is truly just a really good friend. We simply enjoy hanging out together.'

'Plenty of relationships start out as friends.'

'Gran, trust me. There's nothing. And I'm in no hurry to jump into another relationship.'

'A year is hardly *hurrying*,' she muttered. 'You want kids, don't you?'

'Not with just anyone,' Emma scoffed.

And then suddenly Gran frowned, her eyes lit up and she announced, 'I've remembered who that young Mal is,' and told Emma.

'Interesting.' Emma was stunned. 'I wonder why he didn't say? I thought he was just some random tradie.'

For the rest of the week, Emma went into The Stables daily as usual and plunged into work restocking her jewellery supply for the weekend. On Friday, as she finished crimping off a bracelet before fixing a toggle clasp to each end, her thoughts drifted to Mal and his probable reappearance in town. Crazy to be thinking of a man who, for various reasons she had already recycled in her head and should really be off limits, only for her to discover with dismay that she really fancied seeing him again.

2

'So this is where you hide out?'

Emma recognised his voice of course before she even looked up. Even so, the exhilarating sight of him when she swung around was a loaded jolt to her senses.

'You're back,' she squeaked, sounding star struck and immature.

No reason why she should feel so ridiculously happy to see him again or that he had sought her out. It was breezy out today so his dark curls tumbled over his forehead in a gorgeous mess. In jeans, a checked blue shirt and sleeveless black puffer jacket, he looked even better than she remembered him from last weekend. Was that possible? And way too manly for such a boy.

'I drove up last night.' He lounged against her counter, arms crossed over his chest. 'Just grabbed a few weekend supplies. You're right. Tingara is small enough. First person I asked knew where to find you.'

Emma wondered who that might have been but didn't ask. 'I'm not hiding.'

'I wasn't sure you wanted to be found.' He moved position and perched on a nearby stool, wrecking her poise. 'Don't let me interrupt you.' He nodded to the components of a blue and silver bracelet lying on her work table in the process of creation.

Fat chance. Her concentration was shot. Some early browsers came into her stall so Emma excused herself, grateful for the interruption. From the corner of her eye as she attended to them, she noticed Mal slide off his stool and peer closely into her glass cabinets to examine her displays.

After her customers made their purchase and left, he said, 'Your creations are stunning. I can see why women are attracted and men be tempted to buy for them.'

Few people showed such a professional interest. He seemed genuine. 'Thank you.'

'Where did you train?'

'Started with an arts college degree then realised I wanted to become a fully qualified jeweller so I did a four year apprenticeship contract. Split my time between on-the-job training and TAFE classes in jewellery manufacture. I've been my own boss for years now.'

'In Tingara?'

He was probing but she didn't mind. After all, Emma was curious beyond all common sense about his background, too, now that she knew his true identity. 'Sydney until recently.' She flashed a quick dismissive smile. 'Needed a change.' The only explanation she was prepared to give.

'Fair enough.' His blue eyed gaze roamed her collection again. 'You have a flair for bright things.'

'I love jewel colours,' she admitted, 'Old fashioned designs like crystals and chandelier drops.' Without thinking because he was being so perceptive, she added, 'Do you want to see my gems?'

He chuckled. 'Is this like etchings?'

Emma felt herself grow hot with embarrassment. She never invited anyone into her small repository in the vault but she impulsively let down her guard around this likable male.

'Behave yourself,' she snapped more sharply than intended but his cheeky manner was proving heady and unsettling, and she was unprepared for it. 'I rent a walk-in safe for my precious stones. In here.'

She heaved on the thick metal door and stepped inside. A glittering modest selection of precious coloured stones like opals, sapphires, amethysts and rubies hid in shallow felt-lined drawers that she pulled out to show him.

He gave a soft whistle. 'Impressive.'

Emma forgot she always came in here

alone but Mal's questions and curiosity about her work enticed her to share these special treasures. So when she slid the drawers closed again and turned to shuffle out, she was jammed up against Mal's chest.

She gasped. 'After you.'

'And if I don't?'

Emma appreciated a sense of humour as much as the next person but, right at this moment, Mal's playfulness left her breathless.

'It's cold in here,' he murmured.

'It's wonderful in summer.' Her words emerged like a whisper.

'Happy to keep you warm.' He grinned.

'Out.' Emma demanded, panicking at her response to his light hearted banter and gave him a gentle push on the chest. The warmth of his body seeped through his shirt into her hands.

Scowling, he backed away and the tension eased but his comments and frisky attitude expressed his attraction. Emma mentally clocked a long list of cons to getting involved with anyone right now or in the near future, let alone this irresistible youthful creature. Still married for starters and not yet officially divorced. Burnt once by a spectacular muck up, she certainly wasn't looking for a new romance any time soon.

Mal Webster himself was one giant hurdle.

He was way too young. She would be labelled a cougar. Wasn't that the word they used these days for an older woman and younger man? Worse, people might pity her cradle snatching as desperate.

'You're quiet. I've upset you.' Emma opened her mouth to protest when he added, 'You're an attractive woman. You must get loads of male attention.'

Emma had tended to fade into the background around Steve's polished social personality so she couldn't really say she was ever aware of any riveting admiration.

'I'm old enough to be your mother,' she hissed, not ungrateful for the compliment.

'You're joking, right? You're not thirty yet?'

'I wish. Think again, junior,' she quipped.

He shrugged. 'You certainly don't look older. Besides, what's a few years,' he argued, undeterred. 'No biggie. I started work at sixteen, learnt a lot about life by nineteen and in the past year I've been through the wringer. Trust me, I'm a man of the world and more responsible than I look. Emma . . . ?' he raised his eyebrows in query.

She relented, only because he was so damned appealing. 'Hamilton. My maiden name. It's a long story.' Just so he knew.

'I hope you feel you can share it some

time,' he said softly.

'Maybe. And I know exactly who you are, Mr. Webster of *Clovelly* house.'

'Ah.' He burst out laughing. 'Busted. My cover's blown.'

A group of bubbly chattering girls crammed into Emma's stall, gushing over her pieces. Their heavily made up eyes and pouty smiles flashed only for Mal.

'Ladies,' he nodded, edging aside.

They giggled. Feeling ancient, Emma served them but felt validated when she made multiple sales.

When Mal still lingered, Emma teased, 'Shouldn't you be working?'

'Probably. Getting distracted by a gorgeous brunette.'

'Good luck with that.'

She tried to feel bruised as he started to leave but he paused when something caught his eye. 'What are they?'

Emma's prized fat glass jars of beads sat lined up on a shelf. When the sun shone through the skylights overhead, it caught their lights and they glowed with transparent rainbow colour.

'More supplies.'

'Where do you find them?' He lifted a jar and turned it around in his hands.

'I've collected them since childhood.

Nowadays I haunt markets, estate auctions and antique shops to maintain my stocks.' She sighed. 'I know it doesn't look like it but my stocks are getting low. I need more. Unfortunately it means hunting on weekends because like The Stables here, all the markets are on and antique and junk shops are open. So it means closing my stall.'

'I'd be happy to tag along.'

He wasn't giving up, even in the face of the discouragement Emma dished out. 'Probably not the best idea. It's lots of driving and fossicking. You'd be bored and I prefer to stay focused.'

'Fair enough.' He fished keys out of his pocket and jingled them. 'I presume at some point you stop to eat?'

'I can't close here. Especially not at the weekend,' she explained.

'A picnic in the rotunda? One o'clock. I'll arrange everything.'

Emma sighed. The rotunda in the park would be the most conspicuous place to meet in Tingara. Everyone would see them. There would be gossip. Gran would hear. She would have to close her stall for at least an hour. Trade picked up from late morning. She felt *pressured*.

Emma shook her head. 'I'm sorry but thanks for offering.'

He looked her up and down and grinned. 'I'm a patient man. I can wait.' He gave a thumbs up, waved and left.

Emma felt mean for refusing lunch but this attraction thing was happening too fast. Steve had flipped her heart five years ago but it didn't compare to what she felt around Mal on barely a few days' acquaintance. His departure alerted her to be careful. She'd been quickly and easily led before. It wouldn't happen again. She was a different stronger woman now.

Her feelings for Steve had been more like blind infatuation and stupendous sex. She had worshiped him but for Emma, the fast lifestyle and unacceptable behaviour had palled. Every woman who came along was fair game for Steve. Where once she had thought he oozed appeal and was popular, she now knew better. She hadn't heard from him since leaving Sydney. Incredible, but she had sworn her family to secrecy as to her whereabouts and deliberately covered her tracks. The time and distance vital to ease her crushing hurt and reclaim her sense of self.

Now she felt ready for her future. Wherever and whatever it turned out to be. She honestly hadn't given it much serious thought this past year, felt no pressures or demands.

Content to amble along and settle into Tingara's quiet village life. She guessed she would happily bumble along waiting for the catalyst that drove her future options. But Mal Webster wasn't one of them.

★   ★   ★

This is ridiculous. Emma strode out along Wattle Gully Road in the direction of *Clovelly*. Why punish yourself? What happened to pulling back?

Mind you, in her favour, she *had* delayed her appearance. Taken the long way around through the main street, past old honey coloured granite buildings. Sauntering beneath the low ornate verandas with their frills and scrolls, Mate straining on his leash ahead.

She had even stopped to chat to one or two folks she knew, out walking their dogs, too, or on their morning constitutional to buy the newspaper. Gran always grumbled how foolish people were doing that. Wasting time when it could be delivered to your doorstep and you could read it in comfort before anyone else.

But the south end of town eventually called and Emma was powerless to stop her feet heading in that direction. She was so weak! Where was her willpower?

As a distraction, she forced herself to appreciate her surroundings. Shimmering dew drops trembled perilously within cobwebs and the tips of leaves like fine beads of quivering pearls. The last of the burgundy maple leaves were being bled from branches. The black knots on the white trunks of the yellow leafed silver birches starkly contrasting against each other.

Emma looked ahead. Oh how absurd! She curbed a laugh as she approached *Clovelly* to see Mal sitting on his front step. Probably blue and numb with cold. Seeing her approach, he rose and hung over the white paling fence gate, waiting, although she was still half a block away.

He must be ten years younger. Practically another generation. Did it matter?

'Want company?' He opened and shut the wrought iron gate to stand before her.

'Do I have a choice?' She kept walking, pretending this wasn't planned.

'Nope.' He fell into step alongside.

Emma tried not to stare but she grabbed quick side glances instead. He was dressed in sneakers and trackies like her. But where he wore a padded windbreaker and a man scarf wound around his neck, Emma was rugged up in a long wool coat and knotted scarf with a snug beanie pulled down low over her ears.

Only her red nose and cheeks peeped out.

To stay warm as well as keep up with Mate, neither said much at first. They simply paced out along the gravelled road until it turned onto a bush lane through light beech and birch woodland that followed the meandering course of Stony Creek around the edge of town.

Emma immediately released Mate and he disappeared.

'Lucky dog,' Mal said.

'He has more fun this way. Besides, he knows his limits and comes when I call. Actually, he's my Gran's dog.' Feeling protective about living with her grandmother, Emma went on quickly, 'She remembers you as one of John Webster's sons. You have a brother?'

'Alex. He's a nomad. Travels the world volunteering. Last we heard, he's somewhere in India helping teachers support disadvantaged children. In his free time, he explores the local areas.'

'My brother Richard is like that. Aimless, with no real apparent purpose at the moment. He studied medicine and does occasional locum work but he's wasting all that training and brilliant natural skills to just go surfing. He's still independent and single. I worry about him.' She frowned then asked, 'I believe you have an uncle?'

Mal nodded. 'Ralph. Career navy. Never married and recently retired to Queensland.'

Somehow, when the path narrowed and they bumped closer, Mal slid his hand into Emma's. Whether by accident or on purpose she didn't know but it was the first physical gesture of intimacy between them outside the spark and banter. Her instinct was to pull away but she found the warmth and hinted comfort reassuring and too lovely to break apart. She would so regret this. Compared to her, Mal was virtually a teenager but the feeling was so nice, she left their hands linked. And was highly aware of his touch.

'What's the story with *Clovelly*?' she asked. 'No one in your family want to keep it?'

'My grandfather George was a hard and crafty old bugger. Stern. Drove away his sons from Dad's account. Didn't know how to smile.'

Emma nodded. 'Sad. I get the picture.'

'My father left home as soon as he could and Ralph joined the navy of course. Neither of them want anything to do with the house.'

'Pity,' she murmured. 'It's a lovely old place.'

'Yeah but not sure it was ever a home in the true sense. Dad and Ralph always believed old George's rigid attitude drove

Grandma Anne into an early grave.'

Emma squeezed his hand in understanding.

'What about your family?'

'All in Sydney.'

'Siblings?'

'My brother Richard as I just mentioned and a younger sister, Julie. Married with two kids.'

When she didn't elaborate, he stopped walking. 'So, do I have any rights to kiss you?'

'Meaning is there someone else?'

Mal shrugged. 'You mentioned your maiden name when we introduced. Don't expect details. Just where I stand.'

Emma took a deep breath. 'Shitty marriage basically. Wrong choice but didn't realise it at the time.'

'Can I ask what happened?'

'Steve,' she managed to bring his name out into the open between them, 'Was persuasive and, in the end, unfaithful. We're separated. But if I'm honest, it was over anyway.'

'Ah.' He hesitated and a charge of expectation rose between them. 'What if I kissed you right about now?'

'You'll ruin a perfectly good friendship,' she argued.

'Friendship huh? Are you sure?' He raised their linked hands and grinned then grew serious. 'Not big on taking risks just yet, huh? Not ready to move on?' he suggested gently.

Bullseye. How close to the mark was that? She shook her head. 'Just being cautious.'

Really, after a year, should she be more open to moving on?

He pulled her into his arms and just held her. Snuggled against his big warm body it was impossible to get close enough with all their winter gear between them. Emma filled with a deep sense of contentment but couldn't stop making comparisons between Mal and Steve. Hard not to. Mal possessed a much lighter heart. He was fun company and she forgot her troubles around him. But he was leaving when *Clovelly* was finished. What then?

Mal massaged her back and kissed her forehead. Then she heard him utter a low growl. Suddenly, he pulled away from her and tugged her off the path beneath the green and dripping lacy canopy of a weeping willow.

She didn't resist when kissed. Her body responded naturally and instinctively as though it had always been this way. When he deepened the kiss, she stirred with longing. Craving to get closer, her hands stole up beneath his windbreaker.

Emma grew vaguely aware someone swiftly and briefly cycled past. It was a long while

44

before either of them wanted to break apart. They rested their foreheads together. Somehow Mal's big hands had invaded her coat and wrapped around her waist.

'I'm still a married woman,' she groaned.

'Do you feel married?'

'No.'

'There's your answer, then.' Mal paused. 'Did you mind being married?'

'Not at first while I was still smitten until I realised he was the wrong choice.'

'So you won't mind being married again, then?'

They had barely met. He couldn't be suggesting a future? She considered how attuned they seemed to each other already. Uncanny and not a little scary.

Being honest with herself, Emma slowly shook her head. 'So long as it's with the right person next time.' Gathering her common sense together after their fierce and needy kissing, Emma chuckled, 'Mate could be miles away.' She stuck her fingers in her mouth and whistled.

Mal shook his head in admiration. 'Always wished I could do that.'

It wasn't long before the dog loped out of the woods, wildly shook himself and trotted over to them.

Emma checked her watch. 'This walk has

gone way over my usual time. Gran will be full of questions.'

'Have you had breakfast?'

'Nope, but-'

'Hot chocolate?' When she hesitated, he said, 'I'll add extra marshmallows.'

'Very persuasive.' She held up both hands and spread her fingers. 'Ten minutes tops.'

They linked arms and headed back for *Clovelly*.

Because the sun had burnt off the last veils of fog, Emma and Mal sat out on the now sunny front steps of the house, hands cupped around their mugs of hot chocolate.

'Do you know how this house was named?' she asked.

'After the seaside village of Clovelly in Devon in England where George's ancestors came from. It has steep narrow streets down to the water apparently. Looks picturesque. Mean to go there one day.'

'Your grandfather must have had some sense of family and nostalgia then.'

'He never showed it.'

Emma looked back over her shoulder. 'So, when you're done, this house goes out of the family?'

'I can't afford to buy it even if I wanted to.'

'Would you if you could?'

'Not sure. I didn't grow up here and rarely

visited. There's no real attachment for me. And I have enough other stuff going on in my life at the moment. I'm only working on *Clovelly* for the money. I'm being paid out of the estate. I need every dollar I can get right now. I'm only sleeping on the floor so I don't have to pay for a motel,' he admitted.

Emma frowned. 'What on earth's the problem?' she asked gently.

'My business partner stole money to pay for his gambling habit.' Emma gasped. 'He was a school friend. I would have lent it to him for any legitimate need. I've worked sixty hour weeks the past five years to build up my business and reputation as a nest egg and now it is gone. Bloody waste.' Mal glanced at Emma. 'Sorry.'

'Don't apologise. Clearly not your fault.' She looked off into the distance. 'We all need to vent when life sucks.'

Mal sighed. 'I'm a master builder. By association my reputation's not so much shot as damaged. I'd already reported the fraud before I discovered it was Pete. I'm taking him to court but what purpose will it serve? There's no chance of recovering my money. Pete's lost his job and his family, his wife Deb's moved in with her parents, and he has little chance of getting work again. At least locally. What's left for him?' He looked around. 'So I thought if I did this place on my own, high spec, I could use the quality of craftsmanship to push back into business again. Alone this time. I'm not trusting anyone.'

Emma seized on an idea. 'You and Will Bennett should meet. He's an architect and you're a builder.' She shrugged. 'He's an old school friend of mine. He's a popular artist in town now and a creative soul. Might be worthwhile.'

Mal considered her suggestion. 'Where does he live?'

'Gum Tree Lane.'

'West side of town. I'll check him out. At this point in my life I have nothing to lose. I'll give it a shot.'

'You could get together, do a project and split the profits. A new build or another renovation?' she suggested.

'Possible,' he considered. 'Nothing to lose.'

'Okay. I'll ask him then?' she ventured.

Mal nodded. 'Thanks.'

'Might not come to anything but it could prove worthwhile if you at least meet. Will's a great guy. Easy going. Open to ideas. Hides his light under a hay bale but a brilliant designer. He built his own mud brick passive solar home and did the St. Anne's church renovation for Ginny Bates. He mostly paints now but he takes the occasional architectural commission.'

'Young people often drift away from small towns. I'm surprised you and Will are both here. Why are you in Tingara?' Mal asked. 'I know you're separated but–'

'It seemed logical for me right now,' Emma shrugged. 'I grew up here but our family moved to the city. It never felt like home to me. Gran pegged me right there. I live with her by the way,' she confessed sheepishly.

'I figured,' he grinned. 'You've mentioned her so often, she's obviously important to you.'

'Yes,' Emma realised, smiling. 'She is. Young in heart and mind. I feel bad singing praises of a grandparent when from all accounts one of yours was a piece of work.'

'That's life. You can choose your friends — '

'But you can't choose your family,' Emma finished for him, smiling. Families, she mused. You couldn't do without them.

'The few times we visited them here, I remember my grandma Annie fondly though. Always in the kitchen cooking and always wore full aprons with flowers and embroidery on them. Lovely lady. Died years ago, though.'

Emma set her empty mug on the step, stretched and rose. 'I could sit and talk to you all day — '

'Warming to me then, huh?' he teased.

'Don't be smug.' She grinned. 'I need to get to work.'

Mal stood up beside her. 'Thanks for letting me join you and Mate on your walk.'

'Rubbish. You ambushed us!'

The dog had settled patiently nearby but now jumped to his feet, tail wagging, scenting action.

At least one of us is keen to leave, Emma thought.

She was about to move off when Mal asked, 'Haven't you forgotten something?'

Emma frowned. 'What?'

'You may not need another kiss but I sure do,' he growled.

Emma relented as he scooped her into his powerful arms and gave her something to remember until next time. What else could a woman do, confronted by such a charming devilish man? Resistance was a challenge, especially when she felt such a deep pull toward him since the moment they met. She clung to him like a lifeline, relishing his warmth, the touch and feel of him. This man was dangerous, she thought as they kissed, but oh how she craved him, too.

As one of his hands stole beneath her hair and cupped her neck, both seemed reluctant to part. Their mouths sought each other and

Emma's body sagged against his.

'I have to leave early today,' Mal said. 'Late afternoon. My partner's theft case is scheduled for the Magistrate's Court tomorrow. If Pete pleads guilty it will save court time and expense but I need to get my paperwork in order and phone my lawyer.'

'Good luck. I hope it all goes well for you.'

Mal hesitated. 'How about I bring a late bakery lunch to The Stables before I go?'

She shouldn't. This was all too good to be true.

'Come on. You know you want to,' Mal urged in the face of her hesitation, grinning with mischief.

He was so adorable. How could she say no? 'All right. See you then,' she agreed.

*　*　*

Emma walked away feeling ridiculously happy but crossed her fingers. Was it the right decision? Mal was such fun. So different to Steve but so young, she sighed. Was her head being turned by his attention and flattery? No. It felt real. But she grew terrified that it might lead to disappointment again.

No. You're overthinking this, she argued, as Mate pulled her closer to home. Her gut instinct told her Mal Webster was the real deal. Trustworthy. Emma's life in Sydney had at least taught her better judgement of people. So why did she feel like a nagging pin was poised ready to burst her bubble?

When she finally returned to the flat, Gran flashed Emma a mocking smile. 'Get lost again?'

'Held up,' Emma admitted.

'Sounds promising.'

'Gran!' Emma was seeing a spirited side to her grandmother's nature and a rare and uplifting open mind from an oldie. 'We were just talking.'

'Boring. If you really like this toy boy I hope you were doing more than that.'

Embarrassed and speechless, feeling not in the least guilty and protecting her privacy, Emma turned away and buttered toast. Still, as she ate breakfast and readied for work, she worried over this new state of affairs in her life with Mal. Nothing was anywhere near resolved with Steve at the moment.

The word *divorce* loomed large in her mind and with it came the knowledge of the need to return to Sydney to claim the rest of any possessions she might want to keep from the apartment.

And now, just to complicate her life, Mal Webster happened along. After a year since her separation, to experience this sudden heady excitement that would easily explode into passion if she allowed it, was alarming. And made her aware that she and Steve never had anything like it.

For now, she guessed there wasn't anything wrong with letting another man into her life, surely? It might work. It might come to nothing. One day at a time then.

★　★　★

Lunch at The Stables for Emma and Mal was grabbing quick bites of a salad roll washed down with heavenly sips of takeaway coffee.

Mal seemed content to linger while she served a steady flow of customers during his stay. The few times numbers of browsers thinned she noticed he edged nearer or reached for her hand or stole a hasty kiss. All making Emma feel absurdly cherished.

Not a hint from this man of the unwelcome criticism or censure that had been the constant unpleasant aspect of her relationship and marriage to Steve. This lighter accept-ability and enjoyment of each other came as a refreshing change. Emma chose not to examine or regret the past too much, the potentially wasted years, but focused on the future instead.

When it came time for Mal to leave, Emma

noted his reluctance and felt the tug of loss, too.

Fortunately, a party of ladies entered the stall, raving over her glittering jewellery so, while Emma became busy and distracted, Mal quickly waved and left. But not before a reassuring squeeze of the hand and last lingering glance passed between them.

It was going to be a long week, during which she really should give the wisdom of this new friendship some serious thought.

3

How boring and quiet could one week be? Emma wondered restlessly. Trade at The Stables was unusually slow so on impulse one afternoon mid week, she locked up and wandered out to Gum Tree Lane to annoy Will.

Fortunately he was home, scruffy and painting. Unusual for the daytime because he mentioned once that he often painted at night. She sat quietly for a while as he worked and they drank mugs of tea. When he finally laid his brushes aside to take a break, Emma mentioned Mal Webster, his situation and the possibility that Will might consider embarking on a mutually worthwhile project together with him.

Will agreed and almost in the same breath probed at Emma's connection with Mal.

'Just helping a friend.' Emma played down her interest and swiftly brushed aside his suspicion, remaining guarded of her association with Mal.

Emma left Will's house later feeling her week wasn't totally wasted in fretting and pacing. She had at least achieved something constructive.

* * *

Because Emma worked late Friday nights preparing for another lucrative weekend at The Stables, and it was Gran's busiest day in the op shop, their evening dinner was always Chinese takeaway and white wine. Emma loved this night of the week as she walked home swinging her bags full of hot plastic takeaway food containers, watching village life quicken and buzz ahead of those weekend tourists already arriving. Increasing traffic idled bumper to bumper along Main Street and restaurants hummed with more diners than during the quiet weekdays.

Almost home and preoccupied with idle thoughts of Mal, her heart skipped a beat and she nearly dropped the food to see his vehicle parked in Gran's narrow driveway. She squeezed past it, avoiding the prickly bare rose bushes along the path. Mate barked as usual, sensing her approach, and Gran opened the front door as usual. Except, not as usual, their guest hovered in the lounge room behind.

Her bags were swiftly whipped from her hands.

Mal leant forward, beaming, and pressed a warm kiss on her cheek. 'Evening. Let me help you with those.'

While he still had his back turned, over his shoulder Emma caught Gran's playful flicker of eyebrows, a wink and a cheeky thumbs up.

Flustered, Emma said, 'This is unexpected. Been back in town long?' All said as casually as if he was a distant acquaintance and not the man on her mind all week.

'About half an hour,' he murmured.

He *had* left Bendigo early then.

'I've invited Mal to join us for dinner, dear,' Gran said. 'I hope you don't mind.'

'Of course not.'

'He's had such a long drive up. We're already acquainted. You go and freshen up, dear. Mal can help me put out dinner.'

Well, Gran had certainly wasted no time in welcoming Mal into their midst. Emma headed for her room. She let down her hair, brushed it out, washed up, cleaned her teeth and swiped on fresh lip gloss. Staring at herself in the mirror, she knew she looked awful. Too late. Mal had already seen her. With a man on the scene, maybe she should take more care of her appearance? Emma shook her head. Her life felt so surreal at the moment and suddenly changing.

When she returned to the cosy kitchen, Emma heard Gran and Mal quietly chatting together. They stopped as she entered. Noticing the opened containers on the small round table, a serving spoon in each, with bowls and forks laid out ready, she broke the pause with a smile and, to avoid gaping at Mal so close in Gran's tiny flat, rubbed her hands together and said, 'Let's eat. I'm starving.'

The room seemed much smaller with Mal in it. His knees touched hers under the table. They helped themselves and filled their bowls.

As Emma poured wine, she asked, 'How was your court case this week?'

'Difficult,' Mal admitted, growing serious, resting his elbows on the table and clasping his hands together. 'Pete's crime is considered a breach of trust. He acted dishonestly of course and took money to which he had no legal right. Even though it was under one hundred grand, the maximum penalty is ten years prison.'

'Really?' Emma was stunned. 'He won't — ?'

Mal shook his head. 'By the end of the hearing, the judge commented that it was tempting to consider financial crimes less than those of physical violence but they still impact the conduct of business and carry culpability. To his credit, Pete pleaded guilty which saved everyone time and expense. He's already lost everything and been punished enough but the judge said he needed to balance the sentence with rehabilitation. Pete was a gambler,' Mal explained with a shrug. 'But has he learned his lesson? Upshot is I made a submission on Pete's behalf so he was given a suspended sentence.'

'Any chance of recouping your money?' Emma asked.

Mal scoffed. 'Nope. Just write it all off as a bad debt and loss of a good friend. Not sure I could trust him again unless he kicks his habit. I wanted to at least give him the opportunity to try.'

'That's extremely generous of you, Mal, in the circumstances,' Gran put in.

'It was Pete's first conviction so hopefully he'll get his life back on track and his family, too, at some point in the future. Who knows?'

'Well, let's move on to this weekend then,' Gran suggested. 'I've spoken to Ivy Ashford, our local gardening guru, about *Clovelly*. She's excited at the prospect of seeing the old place again as I am. Would first thing in the morning suit?'

'Gran!' Emma protested. 'We don't want to hold up Mal's work.'

'I only have some interior painting this weekend,' he assured them, 'And early is good before I start for the day.'

'If you're sure?' Emma glanced at him for confirmation. He grinned and nodded. She turned back to Gran. 'I can drive you and Ivy around but I need to be at The Stables to open by ten.'

'Nine o'clock?' Gran suggested eagerly.

'It's a date,' Mal agreed.

Mary chuckled. 'You're far too young for me,' and glanced in Emma's direction.

And possibly me, too, Emma thought.

'I'm not sure how much it will help,' Emma spoke to Mal. 'But I approached Will Bennett during the week. The architect friend I mentioned? He'd love to meet you but he won't have much free time to pursue it until after the annual harvest festival in May. He's busy painting for an exhibition.'

'No rush,' Mal said. 'I have *Clovelly* to finish first and I need to build up my business again, solo.'

'Will's happy to meet you any time. He tends to paint at night so daytime or early evening is probably best. I told him you're usually busy during the day but might be flexible.'

'Sure.'

'It would have to be tonight or tomorrow,' she suggested, adding, 'I'm away Sunday,' but didn't elaborate. 'But you could meet Will any time on your own. Probably no need for me to be there.'

'Could you at least introduce us and we'll

take it from there?'

'Fair enough,' Emma conceded, hoping to avoid yet more time in Mal's company, loving seeing him again but uneasy at how readily he was sneaking into her life.

'I'm free now,' he announced.

Emma darted a quick glance at the kitchen clock. 'Might work. I'll go check.' She excused herself to phone Will and returned within moments. 'Will's happy for you to drop around now.'

Mal rose. 'Thank you for your hospitality, Mary.'

Emma hesitated, having promised she would introduce the men but concerned about leaving Gran with all the clearing away.

'You two go on,' she waved them off. 'Takeaways don't leave much washing up.'

They drove out to the Lane in Mal's twin cab ute. Emma felt strange but comfortable in the vehicle, practical for his work of course although far more basic compared to Steve's luxury sports cars in Sydney. Only yuppie weekend tourists drove flashy cars in Tingara.

When they arrived, Will's home was its usual happy untidy jumble. With the men introduced, they settled down to chat. Emma made a pot of Will's usual green tea, not interrupting as he questioned Mal about his ideas, expectations and dreams. Older and wiser Will was quietly firm in their conversation, Mal younger but responsible, Emma could see, declaring himself a fully qualified professional who only wanted to build the best.

When it evolved that both men seemed on the same page with concepts and objectives, Emma heard enthusiasm build in Mal's voice as the men brainstormed, flashing ideas back and forth. She checked her watch and stifled a yawn. All seemed to be going well but this could go on all night, she realised. Will seemed in no hurry to get to his painting. She caught the term *eco estate* voiced and became absorbed in their mutually enthusiastic discussion.

Will was equally as fired up as Mal. The significance of the two men working together was not lost on Emma. Since it sounded like Mal was the logical choice to project manage construction if their plans eventuated, it seemed he was likely to be around longer, surely?

Will suggested they both go away to devise separate plans and do their research. At a later date, he proposed bringing in local real estate agent, Anne Perry, for potential sites on the edge of town as well as marketing and promotion. Will would take responsibility for creation of plans and design while Mal handled all physical work and sub contracts. Finally, the men swapped email and phone numbers to communicate and keep in touch. Meanwhile, Will could finish working on his art exhibition and Mal complete *Clovelly* renovations.

When Mal caught Emma stifling yet another yawn, within minutes he wound up his talks with Will and made polite excuses to leave.

When he drove Emma home, he left the ute idling, jumped out and came around to open her door. With an ulterior motive it seemed for he held her tight and kissed her passionately goodnight. Emma felt herself grow hot in reaction.

'Been wanting to do that all night,' he murmured.

With an arm around her waist, he walked her to Gran's front door. The old fashioned gesture warmed her heart. Made her feel respected and special. A brief mental comparison with Steve was inevitable. Before any social outing, he always assessed and approved her appearance, commenting on anything lacking and expecting Emma to fix it.

'See you in the morning with Mary and Ivy,' Mal grinned, sneaking another kiss before jogging back to the ute and driving away.

Emma sailed indoors wondering what on earth she had started by encouraging this young stallion.

★ ★ ★

Saturday morning before nine, Emma and Gran tried to wake up and embrace the day earlier than normal. They shuffled around each other in the kitchen hurriedly eating breakfast, ignoring Mate's whining to be walked.

'Sorry fella,' Emma patted his head. 'Tomorrow.'

'Rug up warm, Gran. It's freezing out,' Emma said abruptly as they left.

'I've lived in Tingara all my life, dear. I'm quite familiar with the weather,' she replied wryly.

Emma hadn't meant to sound edgy but, since waking, knew her challenge this morning would be not getting drawn even more into Mal's web. Around him, she knew no resistance. So she drove in silence to pick up their other passenger. Ivy Ashford waited at her front gate, apparently inured to the biting cold.

'This is so exciting, isn't it, Mary?' she

chattered as she settled into the car, dragging a large material bag with her.

Gardening books maybe? Emma wondered. 'Morning, Miss Ashford.'

Ivy grunted. As sprightly as ever, she still ran the garden nursery and florist's shop in Main Street that she had done all her adult life. Probably what kept her young and active, Emma thought fondly.

Whereas Gran was neat in a wool coat, tailored slacks and comfortable modern walking shoes, the tiny elderly woman in the back seat had a halo of wild frizzy grey hair and wore a cardigan over an old dress with sensible, if worn, gardening boots. The two women were lifelong friends. Ivy one of Tingara's more colourful characters. There was nothing she didn't know in her field of expertise so she was the ideal person to advise Mal on garden restoration.

Emma parked Gran's car out the front of *Clovelly*. Neither of the older women accepted any help to trot up the path to the front door, their eagerness plain. Mal opened it before they knocked.

'Ladies. Good morning.' His easy smile encompassed them all.

'Oh my,' Ivy sighed as he led them inside from the entrance hall into the adjoining gracious living room, still redolent with the strong smell of fresh paint, finished now and empty of Mal's possessions. Logs crackled in an open fire sending its warmth across the stately ambience of the open space. The elegant old home had risen above its age beneath Mal's skilled handiwork.

'It's exactly as I remember it.'

'Except without the grand furniture,' Mary chuckled, admiring what to Emma looked like a tasteful and appropriate heritage colour scheme.

Ivy squinted at Mal and extended a wiry hand. 'You look just like your father and old George. Knew them both. And Annie of course.'

Mal shook her hand warmly. 'Delighted to meet you, Miss Ashford. I look forward to your advice on the garden.'

'Ivy,' she snapped, handing him the bag she carried. 'Landscaping books from the Victorian era, same as the house.' Her eyes swept the room. 'And old photos from garden parties. I don't need them. You can keep them,' she barked.

No need for introductions then, Emma grinned to herself, standing aside.

'They were wonderful times, weren't they, Ivy?' Mary reminisced with a sigh, either ignoring or accustomed to her friend's blunt manner. 'Grand occasions with everyone

66

invited. People didn't accept for George, of course.'

Ivy flashed her a dark look.

'But because of Annie's baking and the glorious garden,' Mary sailed on then addressed Mal. 'Ivy worked for your grandparents beforehand for months, you know, transforming it all up to its peak year after year for the special days,' she said proudly.

Ivy shuffled with embarrassment at her friend's compliments.

'Took us all away from our own ordinary homes and lives into another much grander world,' Mary added.

'Bloody shame when Annie died early,' Ivy muttered.

Emma stifled a grin.

'Yes. I've only ever heard good words spoken of my grandmother,' Mal said tactfully. 'Shall we go out into the garden?'

They all followed Mal through the house and unfinished kitchen where French doors opened out onto a wide rear veranda overlooking the extensive garden that now consisted of unmown grass, bare trees and recent neglect.

'Humph. It's a mess compared to what it once was,' Ivy grumbled at first sight. 'Course it's almost winter.' She clicked her tongue and sadly shook her head.

'Hasn't been lived in for some time though, has it?' Mary remarked patiently in an attempt perhaps to be fair and soften Ivy's harsh comments.

As she descended the stone steps into the huge open garden, Emma felt for Ivy's despair and tried to imagine how it might once have looked and would be again, she was sure. With an enviable vivid memory for someone over eighty, Emma and Mary strolled behind and listened as Ivy proceeded to describe every flower, plant, tree and item of lichen covered statuary that had existed in the garden in its prime, only the bones of which survived today.

Ivy paused and looked heavenward through the leafless branches of mature spreading trees. 'This was all a glory to behold in spring. In the deep shade of the oak underneath in summer, you hardly felt the heat. Those photos show exactly how *Clovelly* garden used to be,' she told Mal then said suddenly, 'I'll be in the car,' and stomped away to disappear around the side of the house.

Thankfully, Emma remembered she had left Gran's vehicle unlocked. With Ivy's abrupt departure, Emma and Gran awkwardly thanked Mal and said goodbye.

'Ivy will be fine,' Gran said. 'Too many

memories I expect. I'll go after her.'

Taking advantage of a moment together, Mal caught Emma's arm. 'So what's happening tomorrow?'

'Pardon?' Emma suspected she knew where his question led.

'Bead shopping?' he suggested.

Did this guy have ESP or what? 'You can't keep doing this to me,' Emma complained.

'If you say so.'

'You're very pushy.'

He grinned. 'Is it working?'

'You're certainly making it impossible to ignore you.'

'And that's a bad thing because-?'

'What do you want?' Emma crossed her arms and scowled. She knew what he would ask. Could she refuse?

He shrugged. 'My Sunday is free. I'm waiting for the kitchen cabinets to arrive and be installed.'

Emma scoffed. 'Really? Are you making that up?'

'No,' he said easily. 'Delivery's been delayed.'

'A handy coincidence.'

'But true all the same,' he promised.

Emma glanced over her shoulder, worried to keep Gran and Ivy waiting too long in the car especially since the visit hadn't ended well. And she really must open up at The Stables.

'Think about it,' Mal said. 'I'd love to spend the day with you. Text me yes or no.'

'Maybe.' Emma turned quickly and left before he grabbed her for a kiss or tried more persuasion. She was utterly terrified of the situation and infatuated by the man. But she managed to focus and drive the two women home safely, their previous excitement dimmed.

At Ivy's house, Emma swivelled around and asked, 'Everything all right, Miss Ashford?'

'Course it is.'

She scrambled from the car and stalked up the path to her cottage without any thanks or a backward glance.

'She didn't even say goodbye to you, Gran.'

'She's taken it hard. I can only assume she didn't expect to be so deeply affected. I'll go and visit her tomorrow when she's recovered and the memories aren't quite so fresh.' Gran paused. '*Clovelly* was her masterpiece, you know, and though old George was a crusty beggar, she was more than fond of him. Knew him before Annie came into his life. I always thought she did the garden to be near him. But I'm afraid poor Ivy Ashford didn't measure up socially for George so there was

70

never any likelihood she would become Mrs. Webster. Annie proved to be far more genteel and suitable.'

'Is that why Ivy never married?'

'Possibly. Who can say? She certainly never encouraged any other man and made gardening her life.'

'Well if it's true, that's so sad.'

'No need to feel soppy. It wouldn't have worked. George Webster and Ivy Ashford are two of the crabbiest people I've ever met. Couldn't imagine them together.'

★ ★ ★

Later, Emma reflected on Ivy and her lost chance at love. She compared her own current situation with Mal, holding back, denying herself possible joy. Should she seize the day? Life was to be lived, after all, not avoided. Bottom line, she was hugely attracted to Mal. Yes, he was far younger but his maturity and common sense were plain.

His humour was infectious and Emma found herself wanting to see him and be with him. Like any man and woman attracted to each other, who knew what chemistry or hormones sparked it off but she decided to stop predicting or anticipating the worst with Mal. So far, he had given her no reason to doubt his sincerity and readily and openly showed his affections for her. Which she thoroughly enjoyed.

She would take his lead and go for it. Decision made, by midday Emma sent him a text. *Yes.*

Mal replied, *I was up a ladder and nearly fell off.*

Not my fault. Don't paint yourself into a corner.

Time?

Early. Gran's car struggles up hills. You get me?

4

Anticipation of spending a whole day with Mal built for Emma overnight. Which meant loss of sleep. Somehow she pulled herself out from beneath the bed covers before daylight, dressed and tiptoed around the flat so she didn't disturb Gran.

She didn't usually fuss with her appearance when scavenging alone on these restocking and buying trips but this morning Emma drank her mug of tea as she carefully applied makeup and styled her hair. Against the increasing arctic cold of deep autumn, she chose leggings under her jeans, long black boots, her thickest scarf tightly knotted at her neck and pulled on a fluffy angora beret. When she heard the deep diesel note of Mal's ute rumble into the driveway, she crept outside to meet him, closing the front door gently behind her.

He wore jeans, too, with a black sweater underneath his wool-lined aviator jacket that made him look adorably cuddly and above all of which he wore a brilliant smile.

His 'Morning,' was accompanied by his usual instinctive kiss each time they met now that Emma had grown to expect and welcome, flooding her with warmth.

Their parting kisses now, too, were growing longer and more passionate, each finding it harder and feeling reluctant to break apart. Emma huddled against him. Even at this early hour, the sharp breeze had already blown away any sign of fog and cloud.

Mal released her, rubbed his hands and blew on them as he moved around the ute and opened the door for her. 'Jump in and we'll get the heater going.'

To Emma's surprise, Mal stopped at the bakery, left the engine running to keep the heat pumping into the cab, jogged inside and returned with two large coffees and a paper bag Emma opened to discover bran muffins, cinnamon donuts and her favourite almond custard cream bun.

She shook her head and laughed. 'Sunday breakfast. Yum.'

'Where to first?' Mal asked as he bit into a donut.

'I have a map.' She spread it out across her lap, licking her fingers and sighing with ecstasy over her first mouthfuls of bun.

Emma thought his chuckle was for her planning because she had marked and numbered the map in logical order with crosses for each potential stop. Until he leant over and licked away a dob of cream at the corner of her mouth.

'Delicious,' he murmured.

'Focus. This is work.'

She laughed but, honestly, what could be better than sitting up in Mal's man truck, in a comfy seat with heating blasting out over them and the prospect of a day together ahead? The aim was to revisit not only her favourite antique and vintage shops but any new ones they might discover on back roads along the way, besides two listed auctions as well if they somehow managed to find the time.

Mal set his GPS for the first one and they were away.

Emma's day started with finding a stash of old estate jewellery in a junk shop. The owners apparently had no appreciation or nostalgia to keep the beautiful heritage pieces but she knew that with some minor repairs and a decent clean, these would resell at The Stables to become someone's precious possession. Glistening jet necklaces and pendants, Victorian chandelier drops all in delicate feminine styles of the era. She also snapped up some cameo brooches that she loved placing as the centrepiece of her designs.

While Emma hunted out other treasures

— glass and pearl beads were her favourites, jars and often boxes full of them, always drawn by the brightest colours — she noticed Mal also took the opportunity to rummage about unearthing pieces he told her he thought would blend perfectly into *Clovelly*'s garden. In the outdoor section of one antique store, he found two small Victorian statues, a scalloped stone fountain and a rustic old urn that he hauled with great strength into the back of the ute, muttering something along the lines of, 'Ivy will know what I can plant in it.'

At one point, Emma shook her head and teased, 'Now I know why you wanted to come along. It wasn't to be with me at all.'

'You're my main reason for everything these days.' His gaze held hers for a long time. He caught her hand and pulled her against him. 'Finding all this stuff is a bonus.'

In that moment, it hit Emma that she really must accept and believe that Mal was serious about her in every way and, even more stunning, she finally admitted to herself that she felt the same. And therein lay the seat of Emma's current personal dilemma. She could no longer deny being utterly smitten with him. Her initial infatuation had deepened to become respect for the man who had accidentally entered her life and turned her heart from cool to buzzing within weeks. Her admiration for him as a person and increasingly as a decent man in her life had evolved into a full blown attraction. And, dare she even think and feel it, desire.

Always now between them was the natural unspoken assumption that they would be together. An awareness of that growing connection and mutual need of each other expressed in glances, touches and kisses. Quite simply, Emma conceded now that she and Mal were an item, and she would never cease to marvel how it happened so fast.

At first, she had mounted a token resistance, created excuses not to get involved. All of which now seemed just plain crazy. They complemented each other in so many ways. Mal's light hearted ease balanced Emma's tendency to be serious. He was attentive and genuine, quite content to tag along with her and mooch about for the day. She knew his motives were not entirely unselfish because he had clearly expressed his affection for her. In his every movement toward her, courteous actions, in the smallest gesture. If a picture painted a thousand words then touches and glances worked for Emma, too, with equal effect.

Her objections seemed pathetic now and fell away. Her mental comparisons stopped.

In so many ways, regardless of their age difference, Mal was so mature and grounded in reality.

The scudding clouds and frisky breeze of early morning had intensified. By early afternoon, wild winds whipped up leaves in swirling gusts, tossed tree branches carelessly to and fro, and generally played havoc with everything. Flags snapped, people bent against the onslaught as they walked. The grey clouds bruised and darkened, hurling the first fat drops of rain as Emma and Mal struggled back to the ute with their latest finds.

'Time for lunch?' he suggested.

They were in a village that thankfully boasted a small cafe. Emma nodded. Heads down they ran across the street toward it. A bell tinkled as they entered and embraced the interior warmth. They found a seat in a secluded corner, ordering toasted sandwiches and coffee.

Their token conversation was restrained so they mostly ate in comfortable silence. Between sips of coffee later Mal took Emma's hands in his own.

'I've really enjoyed today.'

'Me too.'

He frowned. 'Days like this I wish I lived closer to you.'

'We get to see each other on weekends.'

'That's not enough for me anymore.'

His loaded gaze thrilled and unsettled her.

'The weekdays do tend to drag,' Emma smiled, finding it easier now to declare her feelings since she'd been honest enough to admit them to herself.

'I care deeply for you Emma.'

Beneath his direct gaze, she felt herself blush and nodded. 'I know.'

'Just so you know,' he shrugged.

'No pressure,' she quipped.

He squeezed her hands. 'Actually there isn't, but you-?'

Encouraged by his declaration first, Emma took the plunge and a deep breath. It was now or never. 'The same,' she confessed, feeling girlish and shy.

'This has hit pretty fast, huh?'

'Yeah,' she whispered.

In the future, Emma wondered if she would remember this cosy corner in a small country cafe where she and Mal finally declared their feelings. But what now? What course did their relationship take from here? Did they continue as they were with Mal in Bendigo, she in Tingara and grabbing weekends together? There was a next step to consider. Did Mal foresee it? She wouldn't go there without guarantees.

The answer was reflected in those watercolour blue eyes, drenching her with suggestion, leaving her in no doubt of his hunger. She knew the feeling. An unresolved yearning had built within her since they met. Only now could she acknowledge and feel free to liberate it.

In the following hour as they drove on, an unvoiced tension and need hummed between them. Both completely distracted, neither had interest in their buying expedition any more.

When the heavens opened and rain drummed on the ute roof, the windscreen wipers barely coped with the deluge. The roadsides became running rivers, even their coats couldn't keep them dry and their umbrella was useless in the gale.

Laughing, Emma declared, 'I give up. Let's call it quits for the day.'

'Back to Tingara?'

She nodded, shivering in her damp clothes and shaking out her wet beret, not looking beyond getting home to a hot shower and warm clothes. Emma wisely ditched conversation as Mal concentrated on the slippery road conditions, poor visibility and driving rain that had settled in for the day. Within forty minutes they neared Tingara and approached the edge of town.

Mal pulled over and let the ute idle, looking ahead and scowling, pushing out what sounded to Emma like an exasperated sigh.

She turned to him, concerned. 'What's up?'

With the rain beating down so loud on the ute roof, Emma hardly heard what Mal said next.

'I don't want to take you home.'

He was dumping her on the roadside?

'Stay with me?'

Mal's quiet urgent plea came out of nowhere, unexpected, and Emma gulped back her surprise. He was asking her to advance their relationship to the next level. She wouldn't take that step unless she was serious about him and felt their union, if it happened, had the strongest possibility of success and long term survival.

Instinct kicked in, making her believe it would. Catching the apprehension in his eyes, she swallowed back caution. She wanted this, too.

'You don't need to get back to Bendigo?'

'Not right this moment, no,' he murmured. 'Come back to *Clovelly* with me for a while. Or the night?' he added in soft challenge.

Emma leant closer and cupped his face in her cool hands because she couldn't resist a gentle lingering kiss on his gorgeous mouth.

'You need to get out of those wet clothes,' he growled.

And his hooded gaze told her he wanted to be the man to do it.

'Do you always pursue a woman like this?'

'Only the rare and special ones.'

'Will there be others?' Emma longed to give her heart and Mal to keep it, to be his alone.

He shook his head. It was a promise of sorts. She trusted their mutual attraction and lust would do the rest.

'Then I'm all yours,' she said, her voice unintentionally husky.

'Let's go light a fire.'

Emma couldn't wait for the sparks.

★ ★ ★

As they approached *Clovelly*, Mal turned off Wattle Gully Road and parked his ute in the driveway, close enough to make a mad dash the few steps to the sheltered front veranda. The rain had eased from torrential to a steady soaking downpour.

Mal went first to unlock the front door. Emma followed, removing her boots and shaking off as much moisture as possible before entering the big darkened house. Its emptiness could have been eerie but Mal set aside the guard and relit the fire. When sparks ignited and flames kindled, he added more logs. Then he dragged a sleeping bag over the thick carpet and up to the fire.

He soon produced towels, handed her one and drew the bay window drapes closed, wrapping them in a dim warm world all their own. Emma knelt before the leaping flames and massaged her damp hair dry. Mal removed his aviator jacket and spread it out on the floor off to one side.

'I have coffee, tea or beer,' he offered.

Emma shook her head.

'Something to eat?'

She declined again then whispered, 'I only need you.'

He was sitting beside her, arms on his raised knees, both still and staring into the fire. Emma moved first, turning in front of Mal with her back to the flames. She spread his legs apart and shuffled between them.

'Undress me. Kiss me,' she murmured.

He needed no second invitation. In a heartbeat, his arms were around her waist and dragging her tight against him.

Dozing later, snuggled in his sleeping bag together, Emma smiled into the firelight, musing on Mal's deceptively handsome boyish looks. But his loving was certainly performed every inch like a man. She was blown away and satisfied at the extent of their great sex and realised now that she was already in love with him before they had expressed it in the most intimate way. She closed her eyes and offered up a silent prayer that Mal Webster remained in her life.

True happiness bubbled inside her for the first time in years as she listened to the rain still drumming on the iron roof above.

'You're smiling,' Mal drawled.

'That's because you're an expert lover and know how to please a woman.'

'Flattery does it for me,' he admitted with a chuckle.

Emma sat up and leaned over him, folding her arms across his broad chest. 'I'm starting actions for my divorce from Steve.'

'Guess it will take a while?'

She shrugged her bare shoulders. 'A few months. By spring maybe. We've been apart for a year so it should all go through smoothly. I have to serve him a notice of intention then my application will get a hearing date in about two months. Then it's another month before our marriage is officially dissolved. I've been avoiding it,' she said, 'But I'll need to return to Sydney to collect the last of my things. I left in such a frazzled state, I can't remember exactly what I left behind.'

'What are your plans after that?' Mal's gaze searched her face.

'Honestly? I have no idea. I just want it all over so I can decide and move on.'

Was he thinking about a possible future together, Emma wondered? She thrilled at the prospect. This evening had validated their attraction, pledged their love and bound them together both physically and emotionally.

'I can only take one day at a time until it's finalised and I'm free,' Emma continued. 'But I'd like to believe that you will continue to be in my life.'

Mal half smiled but didn't comment for a moment and she frowned.

After a pause, he said, 'Further down the track, before you make any decisions, there are things you should know about me.'

'Sounds ominous.' Emma grinned, keeping her mood light when her heart felt heavy with foreboding, and she tried not to panic at the thought of possibly losing Mal just when they had found each other. 'Can you tell me now?' she teased lightly.

'It's early days, right? There's plenty of time.'

'Sure.' It was obvious Mal was holding something back about his life but at least she sensed he wanted to talk. But not yet. She wouldn't push or worry. They'd only known each other such a short time. For certain there would be challenges ahead for them but, first, her divorce from Steve.

Mal brought in beer and potato crisps. They munched on them hungrily. As they talked and laughed at the day's turn of events, reassuring Emma about the step she had taken tonight and their potential future, she became aware her mobile was ringing and scrambled in her handbag to answer it.

Mal sidled up beside her, draping the sleeping bag around her shoulders to keep her bare body warm and nibbling her neck.

'Hi Gran,' she answered. She paused and listened. 'No, we're both safe but it's lovely of you to care. It *was* heavy rain and the roads were treacherous.' She listened again. 'Yes it's been a long day for us but I'll be home soon.'

Mal pouted and Emma stifled a laugh.

'Yes, we discovered lots of wonderful things today.'

Some of which she could never explain. The double meaning was not lost on Mal who returned her warning glance with a treacherous grin as he tried to seduce her again while she talked.

'Coward,' he teased after Emma hung up. 'Why didn't you tell her where you are?'

'Gran adores you but she doesn't need to know everything.'

'Why not? She was a married woman once. She'll understand.'

Emma shook her head at Mal's baiting and heaved a tolerant sigh as she reluctantly gathered up her clothes and dressed.

'Can you take me home please?'

'If I must.'

Emma stared as Mal dressed, covering up his powerful manly body. 'You're not driving back to Bendigo tonight in this weather, are you?' she hinted.

'Nah. I'd only be distracted with thoughts of you and run off the road,' he laughed.

'Don't joke about something like that.'

'Sorry.' He leaned across and kissed her. 'I'll leave early in the morning.'

'Sensible man,' she murmured, sliding her arms around his neck and kissing him deeply 'Next weekend?'

'Yep.'

Fortunately, and possibly in relief at seeing Emma safely returned, Gran didn't ask too many direct questions and Emma went to bed loaded with sexy thoughts of Mal and what they would get up to next weekend.

★　★　★

The same Sunday in Sydney, Steve Greenberg emerged from his black Mercedes sports car, straightened his lilac tie and buttoned his dark grey pin striped suit. He glanced up in disgust at the Hamilton's red brick bungalow in south west Sydney not for what it was but what it represented.

He had been appalled when Emma first brought him here to meet her parents. He swiftly talked her into moving out of home and in with him which promptly swept her up into his social whirl and kept her away from them. Thus, he was only rarely obliged to visit.

It had always sickened Steve the way Clive and Alice Hamilton doted on each other. He wanted to shake his father-in-law to man up when he consulted his wife but Alice always put her husband first, too. And look where that had taken them. Nowhere. On a downhill slide all their lives. They were still stuck in the same double-fronter they bought when they married.

Clive had no ambition, no drive, no fire in his belly or initiative to take the reins and make something of his life. How could they be content with such a conventional life?

He adjusted his trendy sunglasses. The area screamed *working class* and dull suburbia. He preferred living close to the city and its social action. He was only here because he was desperate.

Money usually came easily to him even if some of his deals bent rules. He'd learnt from his father who managed to avoid the law but Steve was hungrier for more until his recent gambles and decisions backfired. His unstable finances had all come crashing down around him and he'd dug a deeper hole by borrowing to cover his losses. His so called friends had suckered him, forcing his hand now to grovel for Emma's cooperation. His situation was dire.

He hadn't missed his wife this past year. In fact, her absence had meant freedom. But he needed her now and knew where to start looking. Being a weekend, he presumed his in-laws were home. He could have phoned but he judged a personal visit would hold more influence. Alice thought him a god-damn saint. Any small advantage. Being part of the Hamilton family for the past five years, he well knew his best chance and the weakest link to achieve his goal would be Emma's mother.

'Steven.' Alice gaped in shock then beamed when she opened the door to him. 'What a lovely surprise.'

Thank goodness. Victory. His hunch paid off. 'I hope so.'

'Clive, it's Steven,' she called out behind her.

He hesitated just long enough to be effective before adding, 'I wasn't sure you would receive me.'

'You've always been welcome in our home.'

Alice waved a hand and fussed with her wavy flyaway hair. She was not unattractive and had stayed slim as she aged. In looks, Emma resembled her mother. It could have been worse.

Steve pulled a tight smile. 'Thank you. I'm grateful.' He had no idea how much Emma's parents knew so he played it cool and careful. 'May I come in?'

Alice ushered him into the living room. Nothing had changed or been moved as far as he could see since his last visit a year ago. Including Clive still anchored in his favourite chair watching football on television. Emma's father didn't bother to get up so Steve stepped forward and extended a hand. His father-in-law hesitated, wary, but eventually shook it.

'Clive.'

Steve deliberately remained standing to give the illusion of superiority and dominance but also to appear polite and only be seated if asked.

'Do sit down, Steven,' Alice offered.

He decided to accept — might make him feel more like one of the family still — and sank into a lumpy uncomfortable single chair.

'Would you like a dash of your favourite brandy, Steven? We still keep some in the cupboard.'

'Wonderful.' He beamed his most charming smile.

She disappeared then returned and handed him a glass tinkling with the two ice cubes he preferred. Alice had remembered. But then she had always aimed to please him.

'I won't keep you from your game for long, Clive.' Steve snapped a glance at the television. The crowd roared in the background every time a team kicked a goal. Football was for the masses. Golf at his exclusive club was Steve's sport of choice but he only played with business colleagues as part of a strategy when it promised to be of benefit.

He glanced between his wife's parents and sipped his spirit to brace himself for the coming conversation. Alice would be a pushover. Clive might need more work but money talked and he could always play that card. They didn't know he no longer had much to offer.

'You will guess why I'm here. Emma, of course. We've been apart this past year but we need to discuss our . . . circumstances.'

'Why haven't you been in touch until now, then?' Clive asked bluntly.

Alice's forehead pinched into a frown of disapproval.

'Her choice I'm afraid, Clive. Slightly immature you'll agree but she preferred no contact. I've allowed her the time she needed but neither of us can move on until we address our separation.' He chose not to mention the word *divorce*.

He looked them both frankly in the eye to make them feel included and important. The silence and lack of participation forthcoming he found disturbing.

Steve tried harder and focused on Alice. 'If you could let me know where she's staying?' he ventured.

Clive shook his head. 'Emma made it clear her whereabouts are private.'

Steve gave a practised affable smile. 'I'm her husband, Clive. I need to know. Besides,' he confidentially lowered his voice, glancing toward Alice so she was included, too, 'I would like to give your daughter one last chance to save our marriage.' He knew the Hamilton's favoured the lifetime marriage thing so maybe a false promise would help sway their decision.

'She won't want that,' Clive barked.

'Well, of course,' Alice said carefully, 'It's a lovely thought and would be the ideal thing, wouldn't it?'

'Then I would appreciate your help.' He dare not look at Clive and remained centred on his mother-in-law. He had charmed her in the past. 'You know it would be to everyone's — *benefit*,' he murmured.

Steve had generously helped them financially in the past. Small handouts from time to time because he always remained conscious to impress and knew it pleased Emma. A dinner for an anniversary here, a special birthday gift. Except this time, although he hinted at possible future gifts, he knew there wasn't even a spare dollar coin available to flip in their direction.

Alice frowned and grew bewildered. 'We did give our word, Steven.' She glanced across at Clive.

'We'd be breaking her trust, Ally,' he said firmly.

'Clive dearest, I don't know. Would it really matter? These young things have had a lover's quarrel and we've had plenty of those over the years. Marriage is hard work. It's important to try and keep it together.'

'Only if both parties want it,' Clive muttered.

'I give you my word, Alice,' Steve jumped in. 'You won't regret it.' They were caving. Another gentle push. 'With our reunion, there might even be grandchildren in the wings.'

At this point he would promise them anything. He was well practised in what buttons to push to clinch a deal. When he got what he wanted, his word never mattered.

'We could phone Emma first and get her approval.' He addressed his wife in lowered tones as if Steve didn't exist.

'Please don't, Clive,' Steve said hastily, forcing an eagerness he didn't feel. 'I rather wanted to surprise her. Make our first meeting again something special.'

Since Alice was a hopeless romantic, a characteristic Emma had inherited, he hoped his plea spoke to that side of her nature.

'Clive?' She melted, believing in the impossible and seeking her husband's approval.

He shrugged. 'I'm really not sure, Ally. Steve sounds genuine enough but Emma did insist.'

'We should at least give them the opportunity to try again, dear,' Alice pleaded.

Clive scowled at his wife. 'You really believe this is the right thing to do, Ally?'

She nodded, beaming.

Clive pushed out a heavy sigh. 'All right,' he finally agreed.

Steve rose in triumph, trying to hide it, and heartily shook Clive's hand. At least that gesture was genuine. 'Thank you, Sir. Both.' It took courage but he turned to Alice and kissed her on the cheek.

Alice sighed and blushed. 'I'll go and get her address for you then.'

She returned with a piece of paper. Steve treated it like gold. Before he left, he couldn't resist a swift glance down to check it. Tingara. Grandma Mary then. He might have known yet it surprised him Emma would hide away in such a backwater after he'd exposed her to his kind of city delights for years. He sculled his brandy, waited a polite space of time for small talk, enquired after Richard and Julie, made his excuses and left with a light cocky step. Too easy.

When his high settled, Steve assessed his options of getting down to Tingara.

He could do the hour plus regional flight but would be without a car at the other end. He could rent wheels but he hated the thought of leaving his precious car in Sydney, even in the locked security basement carpark of the apartment building. Anyone seeking collateral for his debts could easily *remove* it so he wouldn't take the risk.

Besides, this might be one of his last chances to drive his fancy sports model on a long road trip. Cruise the highway feeling superior. He had bought his baby new, cherished it and could achieve an excellent resale price. But only if forced. The drive down would be nudging over a six hour trip even without stops. But at least he would be in his own comfortable and luxurious car.

On the return drive to his Darling Point apartment to pack, he cursed Emma for choosing such a small deadbeat place like Tingara so far away. He had never seen Emma so headstrong when they argued the night she left after the party. He assumed he could easily contact her and stay in touch, never expecting she would change her mobile number making her hard to find. Clever girl, though, he grinned. She'd learned some street smarts from him after all. His indifference kept them apart this long and Emma seemed in no hurry to formally dump him but now his financial pressures demanded action.

Steve packed his chestnut Dunhill grip bag for what he expected would be little more than an overnight stay. He only needed her signature after all.

He phoned through to Tingara to secure a night's accommodation. When the landlady, Vivian someone, claimed to be fully booked, he spun a tale of a family emergency, gave a false name, offered her double the rate and she agreed to cancel. Money usually talked.

Then he snatched a half night's sleep before embarking on the early morning run south. He spent the first hour heading south on the M31 nervously checking his rear mirror, suspicious that he might be tailed. If he made Tingara by late morning, as planned, that left most of Monday for talks with Emma and explaining his situation. A nuisance. But needs must.

5

Steve Greenberg cruised into Tingara early Monday morning surprised to see it so thriving. But then he hadn't been here for years. Weekend tourists crowded cafes. He opted to get out, stretch and grab a quick coffee before he tapped in the address and the GPS led him straight to Mary's flat. He'd forgotten the exact direction to where she lived.

He drifted along the autumn streets to his destination. God, the flat hadn't changed in years, he grimaced. Mary Hamilton detested him. He'd only met the sharp old girl once before he and Emma married and again at the wedding. She had instantly taken his measure and they shared a mutual dislike. He'd need to be careful how he stepped. Another unwanted confrontation ahead he was sure. He parked in front, eased himself out.

Persistent bell ringing and knocks on her front door yielded nothing except barks from a dog somewhere nearby. He cast about in frustration. He could sit around and wait. Not his style.

'You'll not find anyone home today in there,' a scratchy female voice called over the fence behind him.

Steve swung about. 'Good morning.' He beamed affably, lowering his voice to charm. 'Mary not around?'

The blousy vision in grey shook her head. 'No. Went out early this morning.'

'Ah.' He stepped closer, thrusting his hands casually into his pockets. 'Do you know where she is?'

She frowned. 'You family?'

'Indeed. I'm her granddaughter, Emma's husband. Steven Greenberg.' The woman surely knew his wife was staying here.

'She can't have a husband.' The woman regarded him with suspicion. 'Her name's Hamilton. Besides,' she looked him up and down. 'You're not the young man she's seeing.'

Well, well, well. Steve hid his pleasure at this nugget of news. This old dear might be forgetful but she clearly embraced town gossip. So, Emma had a boyfriend. He wondered for how long and how serious. Not that he cared. Nothing that he hadn't done many times himself this past year. All the same, his wife's fling might prove useful ammunition, if needed.

'Do you know where Emma is?' Steve pressed on.

The neighbour frowned. 'Who's Emma?'

Steve took a deep breath. 'Mary's grand-daughter. Have you seen her?'

'Of course I've seen her about,' she snapped.

'Do you know where she is today?' Steve repeated, fast losing patience. Honestly, the woman's memory fluctuated like the wind.

'She works.' The woman's eyes glazed over in thought again. 'Forget where. It'll come to me.'

Steve smoothed his sleek hair in frustration. Sounded like Emma had opened up a shop and could be anywhere in town. Seeing this vague woman and her unhelpful conversation was getting him nowhere, he prompted one last time.

'Where does Mary usually go on a Monday?' A blank stare. Steve pushed on. 'Does she have a club or group she attends?' He paused. The woman stared blankly. 'Would she be volunteering somewhere?

She gave a careless shrug. 'Red Cross or op shop maybe.'

It was a lead. 'Main Street?'

She nodded, muttered something, turned her back and shuffled inside, not waiting for him to leave.

As he drove off again, Steve hoped this didn't take long. He had only booked a single night at the best B&B in town and he needed to get his financial problems sorted.

The Red Cross shop was closed but he found the community op shop, managed to snatch a rare parking space in the congested main street and marched inside.

'Mary Hamilton about?' he asked pleasantly of the first old lady in an apron he encountered.

She looked him up and down then shouted, 'Mary, someone out front to see you.'

Steve breathed a sigh of relief. His adversary emerged from a back room and he braced himself for the confrontation.

She stopped short at the sight of him and put a hand on her chest. 'Steven Greenberg.' Her mouth curled.

'Mary.' He came straight to the point. 'Where's my wife?'

She sighed heavily. 'Through here.' She led him into a small tearoom and closed the door. 'She's not around today actually.'

'How long before she returns?'

'I have no idea. Emma's an adult. She doesn't need to tell me her every move. She has her own life to live.'

'Where is she?'

'Busy.'

'Mary,' he growled, astute enough to notice

her crafty demeanour change. She now tried to look feeble and confused.

'Somewhere,' she frowned. 'I don't always remember things these days, you know.'

'Like your neighbour then. But she knew enough to tell me Emma has another man.'

Mary's piercing gaze grew cold. 'What do you want besides trouble?'

'To find Emma. And stop faking. You're as keen as ever. I know you dislike me,' Steve continued, stepping closer to loom over her. 'But I'll find *my wife* myself, with or without your help,' he threatened and stalked out.

★ ★ ★

'It most certainly won't be *with* my help, that's for sure,' Mary muttered after he left. She trotted to the front of the op shop and watched as her granddaughter's despised ex folded himself back into his shiny black sports car and drive away. 'You're going in the wrong direction,' she chuckled.

She had forgotten how dislikeable the man was and still wondered how Emma could ever have been so blind as to get mixed up with the trickster in the first place. She smelt him a mile off the first time they met. But her granddaughter had married him within months.

'Emma's better off without you.' She fumbled in her handbag for her mobile phone.

'Did you say something, Mary?' one of the other volunteer ladies asked.

'Just thinking out loud, Dorothy.'

★   ★   ★

Emma's mobile rang just before lunch as she worked in the relative peace of a weekday morning. Mal would have left early for Bendigo. She reflected on their awesome evening together yesterday in *Clovelly*. They were a bonded couple now with that natural unexplained attraction defying all reason. Despite their age gap which no longer troubled her. She thought Mal was being his usual devilish self and calling on some unimportant pretext just so they could talk but when she checked the caller on her phone, she discovered it was not.

'Hey, Gran. What's up?'

'Your husband's in town.'

Emma stumbled back against a stool for support. 'How on earth did he find me? I told my family in the strictest confidence.' She spoke her thoughts aloud. 'Mum! She always had a soft spot for him. The money, not the man. I wonder-?'

'Surely not, dear.'

'Wouldn't surprise me. Thanks for the heads up, Gran. I'll keep watch. I needed to contact him soon anyway. I wonder what he wants after all this time? He's made no move for a divorce. Must be more important than that to come all this way in person.'

'He did seem rather determined, dear.'

All afternoon Emma looked anxiously about, expecting Steve to appear at The Stables at any moment. She hadn't seen him, nor wanted to, since the humiliating day she left. And now here he was still trying to control her life by springing a surprise visit and catching her off guard. Emma sighed. Her peace was over.

As the lighter weekday trade ceased, The Stables stall holders all gradually closed up. Emma phoned her sister, Julie, in Sydney and explained Steve's sudden arrival. She couldn't believe either sibling would break her trust.

'God. I hope you don't think it was either Richard or me. We'd never spill on you.'

'Of course not but I have to ask.'

'Fair enough. I'll phone Mum.'

'Thanks. It's awkward making calls here. I want to get out of sight as soon as possible.'

Ten minutes later Julie called back. 'Sorry, Sis. It *was* the olds. Steve called on them, spun some story about a reunion and babies so they blabbed. I said you would be furious.'

'Just slightly.' Emma clenched her teeth.

'Mum can be a bit thick and gullible, Em, you know that. And she usually talks Dad around.'

'Trust Steve to be devious but I had to tell the folks where I was going otherwise they'd probably have contacted the police and reported me as a missing person.'

'I would have told them,' Julie laughed.

'Still, it's the principle.'

'Yeah, I know. Sorry about all this, Sis. Call me if you need help or a chat.'

'Thanks. I guess I *did* make it difficult for Steve to contact me but that was the whole point. I needed a complete break. And I always planned to be the one to reach him when I wanted to and the time was right. There's always a catalyst to life, isn't there?'

'Yep. Take care, Sis.'

★ ★ ★

Steve had decided not to waste time driving around town. Mary Hamilton could be mistaken for a sweet little old lady by strangers but no one in Tingara was fooled. She had a heart of gold but a will of iron. Well, he was a patient man. He had delayed this long, what was a few more hours? He drove back to Mary's flat, slumped low in the driver's seat and waited. A private reunion would be better than one at her shop, wherever it was in town.

Drumming his hands on the steering wheel as the car clock ticked over each passing hour, late afternoon turned to evening and the sun lowered early as it did this time of year. Emma must return soon.

★ ★ ★

Mary arrived home from her op shop duty earlier than usual. Steve's visit had upset her and she niggled with suspicion. The sooner Emma was done with that nasty piece of work the better. As she turned into her street, her heart dropped. Her intuition proved right. That Steve. The nerve. Parked right out in front of the flat. Well, he wouldn't get away with this. An idea brewed to teach him a lesson. Might not achieve much but it would be worth the fun.

She didn't look at him as she drove in but deliberately left her garage door open. Indoors, Mary immediately phoned Emma again.

'What's the latest?' Emma joked as she answered.

'Steve's staking out the flat.'

Emma gasped. 'Typical. Always wants the upper hand. Springing this surprise visit is his way of doing it.'

'Don't come back just yet, dear. Leave it for an hour and use the back lane. I'll leave the door unlocked. Keep him waiting.'

Emma wasn't afraid of her husband and didn't see the need for avoiding him but Gran sounded suspiciously excited. 'What are you up to?' The phone beeped from her ended call. She had already hung up.

Mary waited another quarter hour until it was completely dark. She pulled aside her front lace curtain to check that Steve was still parked in the same place opposite her driveway. Chuckling, she took the car keys from her handbag.

In her small car she revved up the four cylinder engine, jammed it into reverse and backed out at high speed straight into Steve's immaculate Mercedes. The ramming crunch and jolt stopped her instantly. The airbags blew out and Mary crossed herself. She put a hand over her pounding heart and gave thanks. No injury, just a nasty shock, so she wouldn't need to pretend she was confused.

She knew there would be damage to her dear little car but oh my goodness, this little episode would be worth any expense and inconvenience.

Steve didn't appear for quite a few moments and Mary prayed she hadn't hurt him. Suddenly his face loomed at her driver's side window.

'What the hell do you think you're doing?' he yelled. He yanked open her door. Didn't ask if she was all right. 'You've completely buckled in my driver's side door. I had to scramble over the passenger side to get out.'

Mary stopped herself from laughing, instead aiming for vague and innocent. 'Goodness me my foot must have landed on the accelerator instead of the brake.' She glared at him. 'It happens sometimes. Was it your car I hit?' She pretended surprise and indignation.

'You know damn well it was.' He practically foamed at the mouth.

'What are you doing lurking in the dark spying on people anyway?'

'I'm waiting for Emma!' he blasted her.

'I should call the police,' Mary complained. 'You've upset me today by suddenly appearing.' She pressed a hand to her forehead as though confused.

'I'll report your crazy driving. At your age, with any luck they'll take your licence off you.'

'I've never had an accident or mishap ever and my local policeman knows it.' She only

108

hoped he took her side when called out to investigate.

Steve ranted. 'I can't drive my car. It will cost a fortune to fix.' Money he didn't have and couldn't easily lay his hands on. All his credit cards were maxed out. His beautiful vehicle would be devalued if a potential buyer knew it had been repaired.

In the glow of her headlights, Mary could see he was fuming. 'Well I don't suppose you bought it unless you could afford it, did you?'

She sat quietly in her car, enjoying every moment of Steve's rage. He paced the street making shouting phone calls on his mobile and swearing a lot. She heard her name mentioned more than once.

Mary fumbled about in her purse and handed over her licence when Steve returned, snapping his fingers and demanding to see it.

The tow truck, ambulance and police all arrived within ten minutes. Tingara *was* small. She knew everyone. The street was crowded with emergency vehicles, house lights snapped on everywhere and curious neighbours emerged to solve the reason for such a disturbance.

The truck driver was also the panel beater so he swiftly loaded Steve's badly dented shiny sports car onto the tip tray, watched by its agitated owner yelling instructions. He would return for Mary's far less damaged and crumpled little vehicle later.

Steve approached Mary and barked out the name of his B&B, thrusting his business card in her face. 'Tell my wife to call me.'

The paramedic checked Mary over, offering to transport her to the small local hospital for observation but she refused.

'My granddaughter will be home soon. I'll be fine.' Mary checked her watch. The one Henry had given her. It still kept perfect time. Emma would be here any moment.

Steve was forced to accept a lift from the police. Sergeant Mills quietly took Mary aside and checked her licence. 'He's filing a report. I'll be in touch.'

'Thank you, Peter. I'll be here and cooperate in every way. I really can't explain what happened. Emma may wish to take out an AVO against that man.' She shook her finger. 'He's her estranged husband and he's stalking her.'

'We'll keep an eye on him while he's in town,' Peter promised.

Within minutes, all the service vehicles had gone, the neighbours drifted back into their warm homes and all grew quiet again on Mary's street.

She shuffled inside. The accident had given her the deepest satisfaction and should put a hiccup in Steve's plans. He would soon rent another car in town, of course, but at least he was gone. For now.

It wouldn't cost her anything except a few dollars excess to get the minor dents fixed in the boot and rear bumper because the insurance would cover it. The whole episode was worth the chaos just to see the foul glare of utter hatred on Steve's face staring in her car window. The feeling was mutual because Mary Hamilton did not stand nonsense from anyone and could sum up a complete stranger at a glance before they even opened their mouth. It was a gift. She had pegged Steven Greenberg years ago.

Mary quietly sipped a calming restorative brandy with Mate flopped at her feet, awaiting Emma's return.

★   ★   ★

Emma packed up her jewellery showcases, stowed them in the safe and locked it. The Stables was empty when she left. After Gran's phone call to delay going home, Emma crossed the Main Street and settled into a coffee and snack at the Bakery Cafe.

As she ate, flashing lights and blaring sirens of police and ambulance vehicles raced past.

She frowned. Must be an accident somewhere in town or on the road out. She hoped
no one was injured.

After a while, Emma checked her watch
gauging she had left it long enough before
going home.

Halfway home, Emma took a break on a
park bench in the evening gloom and made
the dreaded phone call to her parents. It
would really serve no purpose but at least she
could vent her frustration at their disloyalty.
And she was due to call them anyway.

'How could you? I told you in confidence.'

Alice Hamilton sounded feeble. 'We thought
we were helping, Em. Steve gives you wonderful financial security.'

'*Gave*, Mum. It's all in the past now. I earn
my own living.'

'Well,' her mother paused, 'Maybe this will
help you sort yourselves out then.'

'I don't want to be sorted out with Steve.'

'He does.'

'I don't. My marriage with him is over,
Mum, and I'll only be seeing him when
absolutely necessary. His affairs rather left a
sour taste in my mouth.'

'I'm sorry, Emma, dear. Your father and I
meant well.'

She sighed in frustration. 'Fair enough but
know one thing Mum. Steve and I are done.'

'Yes, dear.' She sounded contrite and they hung up.

Not knowing the reason why, Emma did as Mary had suggested earlier and wandered in the dark up the lane that ran along the back of the row of flats where Gran lived. At the gate, she fumbled with the catch and strolled across the small rear courtyard filled with luxuriant pot plants. She peered in through the window. The lights were on and the kitchen empty but Emma could see Gran sitting in the lounge. She let herself in.

'Gran.' Emma called out. When there was no response, she went in to find Mary dozing. Noticing the empty glass on the side table nearby, she gently shook her awake. 'Gran?'

She stirred. At first she looked confused then beamed.

'Had a drop?'

'Don't judge, dear. It was delicious.'

Something wasn't right. Emma frowned. 'You okay?'

'Marvellous. I've had the best evening.'

When her grandmother related the evening's excitement, Emma clapped a hand over her mouth and groaned. That explained all the flashing lights and sirens earlier.

'Gran, you didn't! What on earth possessed you? It served no purpose and caused a bunch of people nothing but trouble.'

'I despise the man. Always have,' she grumbled. 'And it made me feel better. His arrival gave me a shock.'

Emma laid a hand gently on her arm. 'We all need to let him go, Gran.'

'I know, dear. Just having one last spree. He wants you to call,' she muttered, handing Emma the business card. 'He's staying at Vivian's.'

Emma raised her eyebrows. 'Of course. Where else? He loves his creature comforts.' She frowned. 'Steve only knew my whereabouts since yesterday. I'm surprised Vivian had a vacancy at such short notice. She's usually booked months ahead.'

'A cancellation perhaps?'

Emma nodded. 'Possibly.' Glancing at her Gran, she asked, 'Are you sure you're all right after tonight's kerfuffle?'

'Perfectly fine.' She patted her granddaughter's hand. 'I can't remember having this much fun since before my dear Henry died. Oh, the escapades we hatched in our youth.' She sighed with nostalgia. 'Skinny dipping in Stony Creek of a summer's night. My word, it was freezing even in warm weather. Having great sex under the stars.'

Emma gaped. Who was this new person revealing her past, unsure if it was Gran or the brandy talking? Then she realised that of course this lovely old lady had been young once, too. With a life history and memories Emma knew nothing about, so she let her ramble.

'All the more exciting because Henry and I weren't even married yet. I can tell you, the fear of being caught only increased the bliss.'

She was wise to Gran's motives. Take risks. Live. She got it and she already had, despite not yet being divorced. 'Well I'm going to have a splash of the amber stuff myself,' Emma said. 'Then I'll phone Steve.'

'I've made it worse, dear, haven't I?' Gran murmured.

'No, Gran, you didn't. Steve did that all by himself.'

The two women stayed up a while longer, Emma making sure Gran had a cuppa while she sipped her spirits on ice, until Gran retired for the night, pooped but content. She was still unsteady on her feet so Emma helped her to bed. Odd, since Gran was usually so strong and alert.

In the quiet and privacy of her own room later, Emma sank onto the bed, took a deep breath and pressed Steve's number. His unexpected appearance in town was a surprise but timely because she wanted to get their divorce underway and free up her future.

'Finally,' came his gruff response.

'I can meet you in the morning.'

'Mary's flat.'

Emma scoffed. 'Hardly. I don't want her involved or further upset.'

'Her behaviour was outrageous. She's ruined my Benz. Where were you today?'

She ignored his blunt query. Her life now was none of his business. 'Early breakfast?'

Some place private enough not to be too widely seen or heard. Their conversation might become unfriendly. Seeing Steve first thing would get their meet and greet over and done with, letting her focus on her day. After a heavy weekend of sales, her jewellery was low and she needed to make more.

'Where?' he snapped.

The Bakery Cafe was too popular and visible even on weekdays. Emma racked her brain then remembered the new Tavern at the end of the Main Street with semi private booths. Steve agreed, she gave him directions and they arranged for eight.

Emma slid into bed, drained and tense. She tossed and turned, brooding. She was dying to know Steve's *real* purpose for this sudden visit. From what Julie had said, he had supposedly driven all the way down here with the absurd expectation of winning her back. No sensible woman stayed with a serial philanderer. She suspected his advent so far from Sydney had another purpose and she would find out exactly what soon enough.

She sighed, wishing her divorce was already over and finally fell asleep with happier and more erotic thoughts of Mal. Next weekend, she smiled in the dark.

6

When daylight peeked through the slit along the edge of her bedroom curtains, Emma still felt tired from loss of sleep. She invested in a long shower and promised Gran she would walk Mate later. Otherwise she would be tempted to walk past *Clovelly* and yearn for Mal's company when she knew she couldn't have it because he was in Bendigo as always during the week.

Being true to herself for breakfast with Steve, Emma dressed down, not up as she once would have done. Jeans, a soft knitted jumper and boots all wrapped up in her favourite coat and scarf. She merely brushed her hair, left it down and ignored makeup. Deliberately knowing, with a small seed of revenge, she would annoy Steve. He used to oversee quality control of her appearance, satisfying *his* criteria. How could she have been so docile? Because once she had embraced his world and sought to please him. Ignoring her own instincts and wishes. Without realising it, she had lived his life, not her own.

In the kitchen pottering with breakfast,

Gran appeared slow and pale this morning. Emma hated leaving her. She was clearly still rattled after her encounter with Steve. True, the incident was self imposed but at her age consequences were always possible. She was probably worrying for nothing. Gran always seemed so strong.

Emma offered to have her neighbour, Muriel, come in with her while she was away. Fingers crossed less than an hour. But Mary refused and virtually pushed her out the door. Before she left, Emma tucked a small box into her shoulder bag.

Without a car and preferring the crisp morning air anyway, Emma strode out for the Tavern even though she knew it would take longer and meant she arrived late. Well, too bad. Steve had waited a year. He could wait a few minutes longer.

Good fortune stepped in when Will Bennett rattled past in his old clunker of a classic vehicle, an Austin Prefect. Locals jokingly said they reckoned he bought it on a dark night and everyone in town heard him coming streets away. Emma teased him that if he kept it long enough it would become valuable again.

Townsfolk, although in desperate or urgent need, had been known to refuse a lift in Will's dodgy vehicle. Others delighted in the experience, especially the elderly. Anything to save walking. It meant some excitement even if there was a little danger involved, and the potential for later gossip.

Will always claimed he didn't get it for a song, he got it for a painting. Literally. He exchanged a piece of his art work for the car. Everyone considered they knew who got the best bargain out of that deal.

With a squeak of brakes, Will drew up alongside Emma as she walked, leaned over and manually wound down the front passenger side window.

'Need a lift?'

This car that he affectionately called Dora, was notorious for constantly breaking down so it was not unusual to see Will riding his equally creaky bicycle about town instead.

'Appreciate it.' Emma climbed in.

Will crunched the gears and they took off. 'Heading for The Stables?'

'No, actually. Breakfast at the Tavern with my husband.'

'Ah.'

Emma shrugged. 'It's been a year. I presume we'll talk *divorce*.'

Scanning the car park as they arrived in Will's noisy contraption, she wondered what vehicle Steve had hired to replace his own posh wheels that Gran had damaged last night. She couldn't imagine there would be much available up to his standards in town.

Emma thanked Will and they parted.

Once inside and to her relief, she noticed few other diners. The Tavern was quiet with its potted palms and muted music. Locals tended to favour the Bakery Cafe. This trendier establishment was mostly frequented by weekend city tourists and travellers passing through who preferred its more refined atmosphere and rustic country appeal.

Emma approached Steve, strategically placed in a window booth. He would have tracked her arrival. His critical gaze swept her from head to toe as she walked toward him, unwinding her scarf and removing her coat.

He emerged from the padded leather seat of their banquette and rose to greet her. Ever the gentleman. Only for show, of course, to impress women. It usually worked for him. At first. Now it only made Emma remember it was all part of the reasons why their marriage hadn't worked and what lay behind her hurried departure last year. Not all his fault, of course. She had been so naive.

Even at this early hour, he wore a suit and tie. Designer, of course. His smooth dark hair trimmed and styled to perfection. Even his casual dress code on the rare occasions he chose it, screamed panache.

Stiffly standing apart to keep distance between them, Emma acknowledged him. 'Steve.'

'I know Tingara's the back of nowhere but surely that's not the local taxi service?' he sneered.

'Will Bennett is an old and close school friend. He was generous enough to offer me a lift,' Emma said evenly, refusing to be drawn and reflecting, with the benefit of a year apart, on the distasteful man she was stupid enough to marry.

'You're slumming it these days. That car looks unroadworthy.'

'It probably is,' she agreed. 'But the garage keeps it running.'

Emma gritted her teeth and held her poise, choosing a seat on the opposite side of the cubicle as far removed from her husband as possible. Steve resumed his place and a chic young waitress handed them a menu. Emma barely looked at it, ordering a coffee and French toast. Steve, as always, chose eggs Benedict. For a man who took huge risks in his business life, he was a pedantic creature of habit.

'You're looking good.'

She passed muster? Interesting. And a compliment? My, my. Buttering her up, then?

Unlike Steve to care about anyone other than himself. She hoped her glow of happiness after the weekend she had just spent with Mal wasn't too obvious for, while she may be in the company of this man, her thoughts were with another.

'I'm content.' Emma folded her hands in her lap, eyed him directly and leapt to the point. 'Why are you *really* here, Steve?'

She caught a shifty glimmer in his eyes. Her blunt question had caught him off balance. What was he hiding?

He recovered quickly. 'I'm prepared to accept responsibility for our *rift* and move on.'

His explanation was too simple. There must be more. She shook her head. 'You came all this way to tell me that?'

He ignored her challenge and said, 'You won't even consider forgiveness?'

He was distracting her from the truth. Whatever that turned out to be but she played along. 'Not even if you had only been unfaithful the once.'

'My lapse was an isolated incident, Babe. It would never have happened again,' he said urgently, leaning forward.

She hated being called that. Their conversation paused while their meals were served.

When the waitress left, Emma said, 'Liar. I

have witnesses who swear you had affairs with any number of women.' It had been degrading to learn of them from well meaning friends who had held their silence. 'While still married to me,' she emphasised and pulled a tight smile.

Steve's face assumed its usual peeved denial. 'Babe, you know my schedule. I was busy, stressed. I admit,' he shrugged, 'I may have flirted occasionally.'

Flirted! What an old lemon of an excuse. Emma grew sickened by his cowardice.

'We were great together, Babe,' he crooned, leaning forward.

'Once.' While she had still determinedly remained blind, foolishly hoping he might change. Fat chance.

Steve laughed nervously, his meal as yet untouched, Emma noticed. 'We could have made a go of it.'

Emma bristled. 'I wanted more than just a *go*. That's not enough. There's more to a marriage than *making do*.' She paused and said calmly, 'There's someone else out there for both of us. The right one. Not second best or near enough.'

Steve glared at her. 'Yes, I hear you have someone else already.'

Jolted by his comment, she looked down and sliced her toast, giving herself a moment to recover. Appalled that Steve had already discovered such personal information. Furious at the invasion of her private life. She felt exposed and vulnerable but wasn't drawn to reveal anything. Emma breathed deeply and hoped she didn't blush, having no intention to reply. Frustrated over any progress in their conversation, she was about to push Steve further when her mobile rang.

It was Gran's neighbour, Muriel. Emma frowned.

'Excuse me, I need to get this.' She rose and walked out into the lobby to answer it. 'Muriel?'

Then followed a babbling gush of explanations. Emma heard things like *Mary's not well, the ambulance called.* While alarming, it was pointless trying to interrupt until the older woman finished.

Finally, she could ask, 'So where's Gran now?'

'In hospital.'

'Thanks, Muriel. I'll be right there.'

Emma hung up, feeling guilty. She had sensed Gran wasn't fully herself this morning. She should have stayed home.

Striding back into the restaurant, she whisked up her bag, coat and scarf. 'Gran's ill in hospital. I need to go.'

'I'll take you.'

She almost collapsed on the floor with surprise that he should offer but it made sense. Faster than walking, she swallowed her pride. Tingara boasted one taxi which was notoriously slow, at least confirming its need and demand, she supposed.

'I'd appreciate it.'

Steve paid the bill and, with Emma giving directions, they sped off in his shiny late model rental car.

'Where did you find this at short notice in Tingara?'

'I had it trucked up from Bendigo overnight.'

And he was short of money? Emma mentally shook her head.

At the front entrance of the Tingara Health Service building, Emma's hand gripped the passenger door handle. She was halfway out of the vehicle when Steve spoilt his good deed by announcing sharply, 'We're not finished yet. I'll meet you back at the Tavern for lunch.'

Emma's mouth dropped open in amazement at his insensitivity. 'I can't promise anything until I know more about Gran's condition.'

'Midday,' he growled.

Emma groaned. She couldn't think of anything worse but was forced to agree. They had resolved nothing and needed to discuss their divorce. But she certainly couldn't give any guarantees for lunch until she'd spoken to the medical staff about Gran. Instead, she slammed the door and ran inside. Let him wonder.

The nurse at reception knew her and smiled. 'North wing, Emma. She's doing fine.'

'What's the problem?' she stopped long enough to ask.

'Delayed shock I'd say.' She rattled off symptoms like dizziness and fainting coupled with a rapid pulse. 'Didn't she have an accident last night?'

'Yes.'

The nurse shrugged. 'Repercussions, then. Only to be expected, especially at her age.'

Struck with guilt that this episode was caused by her own dysfunctional life, Emma strode down the hall and into Gran's private room. She was hooked up to a bunch of cords and monitors, dozing, her soft wrinkled face peaceful but pale.

Emma pulled a chair closer to the bed and placed one of Gran's warm hands between her own. She hadn't settled for more than a few minutes when Steve reappeared.

She leapt to her feet and pushed him back out through the door into the hallway. 'I thought you'd gone.'

'I did. To park the car. Is she that ill?' He peered over her shoulder.

'Goodness, don't pretend to be caring now. You've done enough damage just by being here.'

'Last night was entirely Mary's fault.'

'Blame an octogenarian. Poor Gran was alarmed and confused by your visit.'

By her own admission, Gran had loved every minute of what she had done but Emma played the sympathy vote anyway. Steve would be unmoved.

'There's nothing you can do here. I want you to leave. If Gran sees you, she might relapse.'

'Don't forget lunch.' Steve barked and walked out.

Emma didn't answer. That depended entirely on Gran's situation by then and any improvement in her recovery. Although her grandmother was sedated and calm at the moment, Emma spent the rest of the morning by Gran's bedside, only leaving it to grab a coffee and use the bathroom.

Regarding the accident the night before, certainly the trigger for her grandmother's reaction today, Emma was relieved when Mary briefly woke, tired and softly spoken.

'I just wanted to deter Steven,' was the only

explanation she offered.

Emma gently patted her hand. 'I know, Gran.'

'He deceived you Emma. You wouldn't hurt a fly, dear.'

'Both of us must bear fault, Gran.'

'I despise him so,' she admitted.

'Me, too.' Emma sighed.

A nurse breezed in, checked her chart and Mary was given another sedative. Since she was under expert observation and would now sleep for a while, Emma relaxed. With Gran safely in care and slowly recovering, Emma's lunch date with Steve loomed and appeared inescapable.

★　★　★

Before she left the hospital, Emma phoned her father to inform and reassure him his mother would be fine, keeping details to a minimum. Still smarting from her parents' betrayal, it was a brief courtesy call only. She checked herself hurriedly in the hospital bathroom mirror before she left and strolled unwillingly toward the Tavern.

Again, Steve waited, looking as city suave and fresh as she was crumpled and strained. What else could happen? Emma heaved a deep sigh and joined him.

She had only braved one watery automatic machine coffee at the hospital during the morning after picking at her interrupted breakfast, so to satisfy her hunger she ordered a seafood stir fry and a glass of white wine.

'I want you to return to Sydney and live with me for a trial reconciliation,' Steve calmly announced.

Emma spluttered on her first sip of wine. 'You sound serious but you *are* joking?' she said dryly. 'How can you possibly believe I've learned nothing from our marriage and would stoop to such a stupid thing?'

She suddenly felt an urgency to cut all this phoney crap and drive her own future.

Steve held up his hands. 'Okay, we're not getting back together.' Emma rolled her eyes. 'So, the divorce.' He hedged. 'That will take a couple months but we need to sell the apartment. Now. Not wait until the decree.'

So, finally, the real reason for his visit was coming to light. 'Why the rush?' He looked guilty and uncomfortable. 'Something's wrong. What have you done?'

He cleared his throat. 'Had a few business deals fall through.'

Emma raised her eyebrows. 'More than one? Unfortunate.'

'I have cash flow problems.'

Interesting. Big Steve Greenberg short of

money? 'Budget. Or maybe try making an honest living instead of aiming to be the world's next billionaire.'

He scowled. 'I'll need time. I'm negotiating new deals.'

Wasn't he always? Emma produced the small box from her handbag and handed it over to him. 'You're welcome to this. I'm sure it's worth a bundle. Sell it.'

He sneered. 'Drop in the ocean, Babe.'

Emma regretted ever accepting the fancy expensive diamonds, a status symbol rather than one of devotion and commitment. Returning the ring meant cutting one more link in the chain that still bound them together. 'And what about that fancy car of yours? It wasn't cheap.'

'It was worth a lot more until bloody Mary rammed it!'

Steven wasn't smiling but Emma burst into laughter.

'My Mercedes could be hugely undervalued if a buyer learned it was in an accident and repaired.'

'So how's that going, then?'

Steve winced. 'Paid a small fortune to be back loaded onto a car transport to Sydney.'

With a pinched mouth and a glare, Steve produced documents for their luxurious apartment sale. She sighed, forking up another mouthful of her delicious lunch. Really? Right now? Just when she was enjoying such a lovely meal. Emma set down her cutlery and accepted the personalised pen he offered.

She scrawled her signature wherever Steve pointed to a sticky note.

'Being a prime property I guess it won't be on the market for long. At least when it sells I'll have some ready cash for the future.'

'I need it to pay off my debts,' Steve grumbled. 'There won't be any money for me.'

Emma gaped. 'That bad?' She suspected his star had been fading even before she left him last year.

'I have debtors breathing down my neck.' He flashed her a searching glance. 'I don't suppose you'd volunteer your share to help get me out of trouble.'

The penny dropped. *This* was the real reason he had come. Not just to sell the apartment. She slowly raised her gaze to meet his. What she saw was a steely challenge. He was serious!

Emma's voice rose in disbelief. 'You want me to give my half to you? Throw good money after bad? You *are* in deep. And you still believe I'm the same compliant woman I was last year? You really do take me for a fool.

I'm not responsible for your financial baggage.' She eyed him with growing suspicion. 'Who are these people anyway? Can't you negotiate repayments or something?'

Steve shook his head, sat back and folded his arms, barely having touched his meal. 'No good. They won't budge. One of the men in the syndicate who lent me the money is pushing the others and I've been blacklisted. They've spread the word. No one will do business with me.'

For Steve, this was a huge revelation. He never shared details about his deals. Emma had always wondered. 'But if they know they're getting the money soon, why the pressure?'

'Revenge,' he went on. 'One man in particular. I . . . had an affair with his wife hoping she would reveal his secrets. He's been badgering me all year.'

Emma's mind buzzed in amazement. After all his supposed business experience and misdeeds with other women, he hadn't learned a thing. 'Who is this man?'

'Teddy Stenner,' Steve reluctantly admitted.

Emma gasped. 'Edward? You jumped into bed with Vivienne? Socialite royalty? She'd never betray her husband. He's too rich. Are you sure she wasn't sent to spy on you? You vowed once you'd never do business with the man. Times must be hard.'

'He was only one of the group. I thought I could trust the others for the numbers to back me. Thought I was safe. But he lobbied every single one of them against me.'

'Money talks,' Emma murmured, sitting across the table and staring at the pitiful figure of a man she once idolised. Externally, he oozed class but inside he was a mess. The former proud and successful Steven Greenberg had hit basement. Well, at least the only way was up but he wouldn't enjoy being on the bottom.

Emma finished the last of her meal and folded her serviette on the table, horrified at the shell of a human being Steve had become. She stood up and tossed a large note onto the white tablecloth to cover her lunch. 'I hope you can manage to pay your half.'

As she turned to leave, he scrambled in his wallet for cash, yelled out, 'Babe, wait!' and followed her from the Tavern.

Emma cringed again at his use of her pet name and the possessive arm he draped around her shoulder when they stepped outside. His touch was repulsive and she slid from his grasp. Only to have him catch her arms and swing her around to face him.

'Think it over, Babe. About helping me out with the money, okay?'

He really was desperate to beg. His plea raised no compassion in her. Emma felt only pity and a heartfelt sadness for the shallow man. Her love for him was long dead.

'No Steve. As soon as the apartment is sold and our divorce comes through, I don't ever want to see you again.'

'We can negotiate my repayments.'

'No! I need the money to buy my own place.'

Emma knew she was raising her voice in exasperation, all too aware they were conducting a domestic argument in public. But was disgusted to see her husband grovel and all for the purpose of the holy dollar. For him it was all about money and how he could use people to get it. Nothing else mattered.

'Go back to Sydney and leave me alone.'

'Babe, you don't know how bad things are for me back there.'

'Not my fault.'

'My life's in danger.'

Emma managed an ironic laugh. 'Hardly surprising. Honestly Steve? I no longer care. Truth is, back then, I married you for your money. I never loved you,' she blurted out, finally able to confess what she now recognised as the shameful truth and aware her voice had raised a notch louder. One couple leaving the Tavern turned and stared.

Steve seemed neither surprised nor concerned by her outburst. Probably because he hadn't loved her either.

Out of desperation or maybe punishment, Steve tugged her close. Alarmed to realise he was about to kiss her *on the mouth*, she swiftly turned her face so that his lips only brushed her cheek. Emma shivered with distaste.

As if his gesture wasn't bad enough, as she stood limp and unresponsive in his arms, Emma glanced miserably over his shoulder. She inhaled a gasp and stiffened with a mixture of surprise, horror and joy. Emma's immediate instinct when Steve seized her had been to pull away. Now she wished she had.

Mal stood further down Main Street having just emerged from a store. The familiar tall handsome man with wavy long hair was unmistakable and stood gaping only a short distance away.

He had obviously caught her embrace with Steve because he stared back long and hard, looking shocked and wounded. She tried to break away but Steve's fingers bit into her flesh and he held her fast.

'Babe, you *have* to lend me that money.'

'No I don't. And it wouldn't be a loan. I'd

never see it again.'

Her frantic gaze swung between giving Steve her distracted attention and peering over his shoulder to watch for Mal. Right now she detested Steve and just wanted to be free. To go to Mal. Her heart ached for what he had seen and might believe. She needed to explain her actions and the circumstances. He was supposed to be in Bendigo all week. Why had he returned? It looked as if he had been about to cross the street. Had he seen her struggle with Steve? Could he have overheard her shouted outburst?

Even from this distance and judging by his rigid stance, she sensed his puzzlement and pain because she felt it too across the agonising distance between them. She knew how he might misinterpret the scene. Be feeling confused. Misled. Her heart bled and she just wanted to sink into a hole in the ground with dismay. She knew how it looked. Emma made love to him at the weekend and today shares a very public embrace with another man in the street. Mal wouldn't know it was her husband and that their kiss meant nothing.

Steve, of course, neither saw nor sensed any of Emma's anguish because he still held her fast. Having had his moment of male power and possibly ruined any potential future with Mal, Steve finally eased his grip. Her impulse to race over to Mal and explain would have been useless because it was too late. Perhaps he disliked what he saw or chose not to intervene but he had already turned and was striding away in the opposite direction. Fast.

Deeply conflicted, Emma pulled herself free from Steve with such force she stumbled and almost fell.

'Too much wine, Babe?'

She wished she'd drunk more but what would that solve? 'Get stuffed. I have to get back to the hospital.'

'You'll need to get the rest of your things from the apartment quick sticks, Babe,' Steve called after her as she began to walk away.

She groaned at the hateful necessity but didn't reply. As she trudged away, her mind spun. Gran was sick in hospital, Mal probably believed she was a fickle cheat, and Steve was broke and begging for her share of the apartment sale proceeds. What next? If every issue wasn't serious, she would have laughed. Life couldn't get better than this, right?

7

After seeing Emma arguing with the other man and suffering a deep twist of jealous resentment, Mal turned and walked away. This was a side of her he'd never seen. He thought he knew the woman but it turns out he didn't know Emma at all.

So far he'd given way to his lust and passion for her but after they slept together, it wasn't just about sex any more. He and Emma had made and expressed genuine love for each other. At least, that's what he'd hoped and believed.

And who was the man in the suit? The guy must be her husband because they seemed familiar with each other, their conversation tense. Even at a distance apart their voices were raised. He swore he heard Emma say she hadn't loved him when they married. He'd frozen in shock to hear the bitter words she tossed at her husband that drifted on the breeze to him.

She hadn't mentioned him coming to town but then neither of them knew what the other one did during the week. So far they both only knew the basics of each other's lives.

Past girlfriends had played him for a fool which usually kept him wary of jumping into any new relationship. But his attraction to Emma had been instant. Hit him hard and fast. Caution took second place to passion. He was blown away by her beauty, her natural humility and goodness. She tended to take life a little too seriously but maybe that was a legacy of all she had encountered so far, including her failed marriage for which she openly admitted and accepted shared blame.

But everyone made mistakes, right? He had failed big time, too. In reality he'd only known Emma for a matter of weeks. There was so much he didn't know about her at all. Which kicked in his own guilt at the secret of his whole other life in Bendigo he'd kept from Emma. He wanted to tell her. Almost had the other night. But the moment needed to be right.

Seeing her with her husband, let him realise she had a past to get over and deal with first. Had it been honourable of him to put the pressure of a developing relationship on her when she had a divorce happening in her life? Besides, he didn't like seeing her in another man's arms, even if the guy was still her husband. If that's who it was. And even if she didn't want to be there. She sure didn't look to be enjoying his attention.

She'd already claimed the guy was a jerk. Still she must have liked him enough once. He couldn't be all bad.

Mal frowned as he reached his parked ute and climbed inside, wondering if maybe he should have crashed the conversation. Maybe Emma had needed his help. To be rescued? Damn. He thumped the steering wheel. Now *he* felt like a jerk. A man who hadn't protected his woman. From a distance, it had been a pleading look he'd seen in her eyes as she glanced over the guy's shoulder.

But, bottom line, Emma still had a husband in her life. He needed to stay out of the picture and back off while that happened, and before he and Emma explored their attraction deeper in the future. He had someone else in his life to consider, too.

No. Best to call a halt with Emma for now and see how their separate lives played out. She might decide he wasn't for her after all and not even want to stay in the area.

Damn. He should have followed reason before getting in so deep with her. He'd been wrong to lay pressure on her because of his own strong feelings. Even though he suspected she felt the same, maybe he'd pushed too hard. Been too keen too soon.

He questioned how he and Emma ever had any chance of getting together in a long term relationship, and how he was supposed to know it was genuine love on her part? How could you prove and believe what the other person told you? If Emma didn't marry for love last time, what guarantee was there for him she had real feelings either.

Mal was frustrated. Damn. Now he was second guessing his own strong feelings. How crazy was that? He hoped he hadn't blown his chance with Emma but he needed to be sensible and back off.

If they were meant to be together, it would happen. He was a strong believer in fate. As much as it would bleed him, he'd have to hurt Emma and tell her they needed to take a breather from each other. She'd object but if he played it cool he could do it. Hadn't she told him he was mature for his age? Well, now was his chance to prove it with some action.

* * *

Even though Emma had told Steve she was going to the hospital, she was torn between visiting Gran or finding Mal. Why was he in town anyway? Was he still around at *Clovelly* or had he shot through in disgust? She could hardly blame him. Maybe he'd turned away to give Emma space and privacy. Done them the courtesy of not intruding.

But they were lovers, her mind screamed out in frustration. They were truly connected now and cared deeply for each other. You didn't ignore someone you were intimate with. You at least acknowledged them. But Mal wasn't a coward. He was gutsy. He'd faced Gran with ease and she could be scary. Look what she'd done to Steve's car. And landed herself in hospital as a result. Thinking of Gran, Emma's steps turned in that direction first.

Mal next. She only hoped he was still around. She wouldn't sleep until they talked.

It seemed longer since Emma had left the hospital and yet it was barely two hours ago. So much had happened and changed in that short space of time. Steve's shady situation and Mal's unexpected appearance.

Her mind buzzed with distraction as she poked her head around Gran's door and entered her hospital room. Her grandmother was awake and half sitting up, the bedside tray table pulled up in front.

'This is a nice surprise.' Emma leaned over and kissed her forehead.

Gran paused in sipping soup. 'I'm feeling much better. They keep drugging me to make me sleep. I'd feel a lot better in my own bed.'

'It's for your own good.'

'I was getting hungry. I didn't take the last

lot of tablets. Spat them out after the nurse left. And all I got for my trouble was this bowl of watery stuff. I'd love a steak.'

Emma clicked her tongue. 'You're impossible.'

'It's lovely to see you, dear. How's your day been?' Before Emma could reply, she added knowingly, 'Can't be going well. You look bothered. Him?'

Now there's an apt description, Emma thought.

'Steven?'

She nodded and almost burst into tears with exhaustion but swallowed back her emotions and blurted out all the sordid details of her upsetting lunch encounter with Steve, his money problems and revelations of potential bankruptcy and poverty, and the need for the quick sale of their apartment to cover his losses.

'You've had a narrow escape, my dear. Count your blessings and be grateful it's almost over. You'll be wiser next time.'

Gran's comment made Emma think of Mal. She was anxious to see him but equally needed answers to her questions regarding Gran's health and situation.

When Emma dared to query her, the stubborn old lady merely snapped, 'Rubbish. I don't need special care. A good night's rest is all I needed and I've had that here.'

Emma shook her head in doubt and warned, 'I'll be watching you closely when you get home. How long are they keeping you in?'

'Too long,' Gran grumbled and slurped more soup.

Emma made a mental note to enquire on her way out.

All the same, she was pleased to see Gran still had her spirit and her wicked sense of humour. It hit Emma amid all that was happening in her life right now that the dearly loved soul wasn't getting any younger. It didn't bear thinking about.

After leaving Gran, wanting to stay longer but impatient to leave, Emma talked to the medical staff at the hospital and learned that, if all continued well, Gran would be discharged in the morning. Which gave her time to seek out Mal.

Gran's car was not yet repaired so they were without a vehicle for at least a week. They could rent one or beg a loaner from the garage but it was therapeutic to walk at any time of year in Tingara. Especially now in autumn, her favourite season, and the coming winter. So she took a gamble on Mal still being around and strode out for *Clovelly* on Wattle Gully Road, sick in the stomach at the thought of her uncomfortable conversation ahead.

But she must face him and explain. It frightened her to acknowledge that he was the most important person in her life right now — as much as she adored Gran and loved her siblings and parents, even though the latter were mostly absent from her life these days. Mal deserved her honesty to set the record straight in case he held any misconceptions about her meeting with Steve.

★ ★ ★

Before Emma reached *Clovelly*, she glimpsed Mal's white ute parked in the driveway. She didn't know whether to weep in gratitude or fear. Her heart kicked over faster. He was still here. Setting aside a swift bout of cold feet and a serious desire to turn and run, Emma gripped her remaining shreds of courage and strode up the front path and steps to knock on the freshly painted front door. A dark shade of green that complemented the white house and garden in progress. The overgrowth had been cleared away to what she guessed was the bones of its original basic Victorian design. Groundworks had begun ready for the lawn restoration and new plantings. It promised to become a beautiful old family home again like the one Gran and Ivy Ashford remembered.

There was no response to her knocking so Emma tried again. This time, heavy footsteps approached and paused before the door was slowly opened. They stared at each other for a long while and neither spoke. Mal's gaze was filled with accusation.

Emma swallowed hard and began. 'I was surprised to see you. I presumed you were in Bendigo.'

'Obviously.'

It was the first time she had ever heard malice in his voice. His blunt response hurt but she had never received one from him before. He was usually so full of fun and easy going. He was hurting. She got that.

'I'm here to explain. Do you want to listen and hear my version?'

'Do I have a choice?'

'I'd prefer you were willing.'

'Okay but make it quick. The landscapers will be here soon.'

Ouch. He wasn't rolling out the welcome mat today. He stepped aside, allowing her to enter. It was impossible for Emma's gaze not to stray to the left into the sitting room where they had made love. Mal followed her gaze. Was he thinking the same?

She tried not to feel abandoned and buried

his rebuff and attitude. He really was taking this hard. On the other hand, it suggested he cared and held feelings. Which gave her hope. Right now, she'd cling to anything.

'Is that why you returned? For the gardeners?'

He nodded. 'Through here.'

He led her into the kitchen. Emma's gaze widened as she glanced appreciatively about. All the cupboards were fitted and gleaming new appliances installed, including an Aga range.

'Wow. This is lovely.'

Mal remained cool and unresponsive. So unlike him, Emma felt lost. He was usually a funny and passionate man. He seemed determined to make this difficult. Feeling awkward, not knowing how or where to begin, Emma jammed her hands into the back pockets of her jeans and leant against a counter, feeling like a naughty child being called to account before a parent.

'You saw me,' she accused, 'And didn't come over.'

'You were busy.'

Emma shrugged off his implication. 'It was only Steve, my soon-to-be ex.' All the same she must press on carefully. Mal was hurting, clearly offended by what he'd seen. 'I don't want to flatter myself to think you might be jealous. If so, you mustn't be. There's no need. Steve is no longer important in my life. Truth to tell, he hasn't been for a couple years. He means nothing to me any more. His sudden unwelcome appearance and my encounter with him in the street back there only confirmed that and left me cold.' She paused. 'But he's still my husband and we have things to resolve.'

'Then maybe we jumped in too soon.'

He had regrets? They stared across the kitchen at each other over another awkward silence. 'Steve and I are separated. We're over. He won't be in my life much longer.'

'You looked pretty cosy.'

'We're nothing to each other.' Emma worried that Mal should think ill of her.

Mal hesitated. 'You and your husband, or you and me?'

You and me? First there was the jolt that he should even question who she meant. And then, the knowledge sank in. Mal was already thinking of them as an item. She'd dared not hold similar hopes and thoughts herself.

'Steve and I naturally.' Had he deliberately misunderstood to sound her out? 'You already know my marriage is over and I'm getting a divorce,' she sighed. 'Steve arrived in town unexpectedly late yesterday after you left. He needed me to sign documents to sell our Sydney apartment. That's all,' she announced with a shrug. 'There have been a few dramas as a result. Gran's in hospital.'

Emma was reassured to see Mal's previous indifferent focus sharpen and he frowned. 'Is she okay? What happened?'

'She's fine now.' She briefly explained the accident. 'They just kept her in overnight for observation. The shock of seeing Steve again. She'll be home in the morning.'

Emma hesitated to let that news sink in and see Mal's reaction. His relaxed stance hinted that perhaps he was more receptive now, easing her own tension. 'I was surprised to see Steve. We haven't been in touch all year.'

After another loaded pause, Emma was at her wit's end of explanations. How much more reassurance and convincing did he need?

Finally Mal contributed to the conversation. Glaring and in a low voice, he said, 'I overheard you say you didn't love Steve yet you married him. What kind of false standard is that?'

Emma swallowed back dismay at the challenge in his eyes and voice. So, he *had* heard the argument with Steve and it *did* sound awful but it was the truth. She took a deep breath and attempted to explain.

'I know now that I loved Steve for a while,' she said quietly, 'But I wasn't *in love* with him. At the time, I didn't understand the difference. Now I know it wasn't enough. I was born and raised here in Tingara. After we moved to Sydney, I still led a close family life in the suburbs. I had boyfriends, dates and a social life while I studied and trained but when I met Steve, I was star struck. He was the opposite of anyone I'd ever met.'

She rubbed her arms and her voice lowered. 'I knew he was trouble, had a shady reputation and appreciated women. But I was completely smitten. He was so damned charismatic and I was swept up into his world with starry eyes.

'I was sick of being poor and struggling. Dad rarely worked or made much money, usually losing it all on another wild scheme or venture. The whole time my sister and brother and I were growing up, our mother worked long hours and many part time jobs to pay the bills and Dad's debts, and put food on the table. Simple fact was, Steve offered the security I never had.' She gave a short laugh. 'My selfish naive youth has come back to bite me. The rich man I married is now deep in debt, people breathing down his neck for their money and he's as good as broke. Money was the temptation for both of us, each for different reasons and neither of them sound. Me for the assurance and safety it meant and Steve for the lifestyle he craved, following in his father's footsteps. He has nothing now.'

'Feeling sorry for him?'

Emma shrugged. 'Not particularly. He created his own downfall. I'm not making excuses, Mal. I just hope you can try to understand and believe my excitement and emotions at the time and why I married Steve.' She looked away. 'It was the worst thing I've ever done.' She turned back to him again. 'I'm older than you, exposed to some less than splendid life's experiences. I warned you off,' she smiled, 'But you persisted.'

Mal didn't crack even the hint of a smile. Emma scrambled desperately for something else to say.

'I'm ashamed of the decision I made back then but I don't feel guilty for not truly loving Steve. He didn't love me either. I was simply an adornment on his arm. When I scrubbed up I didn't look too shabby. 'Course you wouldn't know that now. The way I dress.' She grinned, trying to lighten the heavy conversation.

Although Mal remained silent, he had his arms and legs crossed studying her from the other side of the kitchen. At last he asked quietly, 'Do you miss it?'

'Sorry?'

'The lifestyle in Sydney?'

Emma took offence. 'Would I have lived in Tingara for a year if I did? Of course not but if you *really* knew me, you wouldn't have asked. Steve liked expensive cars. I took public transport.' She glanced out across the leaf strewn rear garden and reflected aloud. 'He wanted an Aston Martin but the price tag made him sweat. Damn tricky getting in and out of that showy little black Mercedes in evening dresses I can tell you. And there was no room for a car seat in the back. Not that he wanted a family.' She almost choked on the admission and tears threatened.

Perhaps sensing her vulnerability, Mal said gently, 'I'm sorry it didn't work out.' It sounded like he meant it.

'Story of my life.' Emma waited for him to tell her she was forgiven, that they could get past this and move on. Together. When no further offer or conversation followed, she pulled a tight smile. 'That's all I came for. To explain. Thanks for at least listening. I should . . . um . . . go.' She motioned vaguely toward the door.

As she moved to leave, Mal straightened and approached her. Hope built in her heart as she waited to hear what he might say.

'I've already run *us* through my mind a dozen times.' He seemed conflicted. 'Maybe it's best if we take a break from each other for a while.'

Emma had not expected anything like this. 'A break?' she snapped, dying inside. 'And best for who?'

Mal stood cool and unmoved by her blunt question. 'I have a lot to do here. Working to a deadline before the auction. I should get on with it.'

Emma wrung her hands nervously together. This was it? She was stunned. She didn't expect open arms, a kiss and making out but he could at least have given her the benefit of the doubt. Shown some compassion.

'I'm sorry I disappointed you. Being an older woman,' she laughed at herself, 'You probably expected higher standards. Keep in touch?' she suggested bravely.

'I have your number.'

'Of course.'

And so they left it at that. Emma felt gutted as she blindly stumbled through the lovely old house, her eyes misting over, knowing it would be for the last time. Clearly Mal didn't truly love her then either because he'd made his disgust plain enough that she had married Steve without love. He had thought less of her for it and dumped her. Shit. She wanted to swing around and cry out *Haven't you ever made a mistake?* but she would never beg him to change his mind. Fair enough. He had his own life to live. Right person wrong time perhaps.

But, damn it. It had been awesome while it lasted. And she refused to regret one single moment even if he did. She didn't want anyone else in her life now or ever. After the divorce, she would live on memories, that's what she would do. Maybe he *was* too young for her after all and the cougar thing didn't matter any more.

*   *   *

Mal stood at the sitting room window watching Emma trudge away as though pushing through heavy snow and not walking along the solid leafy path back into town. His heart ached for her and it looked like she was swiping at those tears that had trembled on her eyelashes before she left. He knew the depth of what he had done. He'd seen the question in those beautiful shocked brown eyes challenge him to explain and give her the truth but he had only stood like a statue and held his tongue.

He had left the door open if he discovered he couldn't live without her. He knew the answer to that possibility already but after what he had just done to her, would she take him back?

Right now he needed time to process what he'd seen, the reality of Emma's life still tied to another. He had already realised he couldn't share her while her divorce was underway. They needed time.

* * *

Emma's mind spun with thoughts as she walked away from *Clovelly*. Mal had told her at the end of their day trip together last Sunday scouting auctions and sales that he didn't want to leave her. Wanted her in his life. Now he's dumping her? What happened to all that passion? Did it just dissolve into thin air? And if so, why? That was a question only he could answer and he wouldn't give it.

From the beginning, he had sounded so sincere. *He* had pursued *her* and, boy, his lovemaking sure had her convinced. Was his rejection purely because of what he had overheard her tell Steve? She had explained the reason and why it was the truth. Or was he being principled until she was officially divorced? In which case, surely there was no need for them to split. Personally, she hardly felt that mattered. They had already both willingly stepped into a relationship knowing that her divorce was in the wings. She couldn't fathom how that should affect them when they were already a couple.

Well, if splitting was what Mal wanted, she must wear his decision. She hated it. She felt like a horrid rejected person but she would hold her head high. She had only ever been honest with Steve and Mal, admitted her failures. Funny that, because early in her association with Mal she was convinced he was the upright kind of man who would accept her for herself.

It was a hard jolt knowing he bailed out at the first hurdle between them. If you could even call it that. Emma thought of it as simply a misunderstood conversation. Mal's actions didn't connect with the man she thought she was getting to know so well.

Emma groaned out loud, shook her head against the blues and stubbornly stamped one foot in front of the other as she blundered on, finally letting her checked tears stream down her cheeks. Looking and feeling like a mess, if she ran into anyone she knew now, she'd be mortified. So she kept her head down, wanting to hide from the world as her steps led her toward the flat.

Mal had dumped her. The mantra repeated itself in her head as she let herself into Gran's place and tossed the keys onto the kitchen table. The gorgeous man she was falling in love with. The man she had given her body to without a second thought because she trusted him, and because of what had sprung into life and grown between them. Now all that was over before it had barely begun.

Mate followed her around the flat, clearly feeling lost and neglected too in Gran's absence and perhaps sensing Emma's misery. Hating herself for being so sentimental, she fingered through all the lovely treasures she bought, reflecting on that beautiful day's outing with Mal, and on the even more beautiful night that followed. God, he'd been a great lover. How was she supposed to forget that? Gentle and considerate but boy, when he got going he sure knew how to please a woman. It either came naturally to him or he'd taken lessons.

Working through a few glasses of wine, Emma decided that until her divorce was finalised, she needed time to lick her wounds over Mal and accepted she was content in Tingara. She had resettled comfortably into town life here, renewed the old acquaintances that still remained and made some new ones. It came to her that she could stay. Permanently. Crazy but the idea appealed. She had enough savings for a deposit on a small house. Her jewellery business was growing, she could afford repayments on a mortgage and when the Sydney apartment sold, she could buy a new place outright.

And she would still be in town to watch out for Gran. Why not? She drained the last of her wine and poured another, settling back into a recliner, absently scratching Mate's head as he sat on the floor alongside.

If she found a place she liked, maybe the real estate agent, Anne Perry could arrange a lease so she could live and rent it for a few months until the Sydney property money came through. At the moment her life and business hummed along nicely even if her romantic and personal life was a disaster zone. There was no need to leave. The security of staying in familiar surroundings was comforting. For now. In a few years, if she grew restless or felt the need to move on, she could.

Feeling at least a little distracted by her thoughts of a possible future, if not cheerful in the light of the one miserable event of the day, Emma focused on what she wanted. A home. A family. Well she could do something about the former. The latter could wait. Seems like she couldn't get any relationship to work these days. Her marriage and quick hot romance with Mal had both fallen through. So she would forget about love and simply focus on being content with who and where she was. Although how that was supposed to happen without Mal . . .

She checked herself. Enough!

8

Next morning, Emma strolled into Anne Perry's estate agency office on her way to collect Gran from hospital. Will Bennett had kindly offered to meet her there and agreed to provide transport home.

Barney at the garage had told her the nasty dent in Mary's car was panel beaten out and would be resprayed and ready in a few days. Emma didn't bother with a rental vehicle. She was happy to walk everywhere. Besides, it would limit Gran's movements, forcing her to stay close to home and take a much needed rest.

No one was more surprised than Anne when Emma greeted her with a smile, leant on the counter and asked, 'So what properties are up for sale in Tingara at the moment?'

When Anne's surprise passed and she gathered her wits, she cheekily suggested *Clovelly?*

Emma scrunched up her nose. 'Bit big.'

Besides, there were too many beautiful and sad memories wrapped up in that house that no one else except she and Mal knew about. Plus it was the Webster family home. She wanted her own place. She knew that now. One *she* loved, one *she* wanted, and one *she* chose. Not Steve's choice of a boxy but swanky apartment with a spectacular harbour view and not someone else's ancestral residence

'Anything smaller?' Emma asked hopefully, explaining what she sought.

Anne frowned and flipped through her listings. 'I have some prospects. How about this morning I set up a few appointments and viewings for you then pick you up this afternoon once you have Mary resettled at home and we can go take a look?'

'Perfect.'

Will was parked at the front hospital entrance waiting for Emma as she arrived. Once Gran was sorted and her discharge organised and approved, amid grumbles of independence and protests of *I'm just fine* if anyone attempted to help her, they bundled her up in a warm coat and scarf and rolled her out in a wheelchair to Will's car. Gran sat in the front seat alongside him, looking suitably royal, while Emma squeezed herself into the back.

Back at the flat, Emma assured Will she and Mary would be fine so with a cheery wave and smile he puttered away down the street. Gran suffered being coddled with a rug about her knees beside the fire, the television on and a steaming bowl of vegetable soup and noodles Emma prepared. She had considered opening a tin of something from the pantry but decided keeping busy was a more sensible option at the moment.

Gran glanced her way suspiciously a few times but said nothing, possibly because Emma announced her decision to stay in Tingara and buy her own place which proved a distraction of sorts.

'Just for the time being.'

'It's not because of me is it, dear?' Gran frowned.

'Not solely, no. I love it here and I really do want to stay.'

'If you're sure.'

No mention was made of Mal for which Emma was quietly grateful. Soon after lunch, Anne Perry pulled up in her smart little car with its bold agency logo and whisked Emma off to look at houses.

First up was *Lakeside* on Stony Creek Way, a cute mud brick cottage on acreage on the edge of town.

'It's only small but in great condition. Depending on whether you're a handy person or not you could upgrade and move on. Great resale value,' Anne suggested. 'The elderly lady owner died so it needs some renovation inside.'

'Lots to look after,' Emma sighed, standing on the lane looking at its overgrown garden and daunted by the amount of work. She had hoped for something smaller and closer to town, both for convenience and her budget.

A quick whip around the property, inside and out, confirmed her decision.

'No?' Anne smiled as they both looked back at it. 'Guess what else just came onto the market? You know the blacksmith's cottage?'

Emma frowned, trying to remember it. 'The bluestone place that backs onto the creek?' Anne nodded. 'It must be one of the oldest buildings in town.'

'1870s,' Anne confirmed.

'Goodness, is it habitable? I didn't think anyone lived there.'

'Tenants in recent years. Needs TLC but its bones are superb and it has potential to be a cosy little home.' Anne tilted her head and eyed Emma directly. 'Something tells me it just might be your thing. Can't hurt to go check it out. Nothing to lose,' she pressed. 'The owner might be prepared to rent while you make up your mind or find something else. Lots of options,' she rambled on optimistically. 'Make a great holiday shack.'

Emma chuckled. 'Shack. That bad, huh?'

Anne smiled, serenely confident. 'Ten minutes. A quick look?'

Emma shook her head. 'Anne Perry you're too persuasive. Okay.'

'I do love my job and I know every single property in town,' Anne enthused as they trotted back to her car. 'I always try to match people with a property. I can usually tell if they're going to *fit*.'

'Anne Perry,' Emma growled no more than five minutes later, 'I can't believe you lied. It's most definitely *not* a shack. It's anything but. It's actually quite — charming.'

Emma peered through the windscreen as they approached and alighted from the vehicle, staring at the blacksmith's cottage. Granted it was small but she didn't need big. She moved closer, standing at the front gate with a hand on the latch beneath a lattice timber arch. Before them stood a perfectly symmetrical stone cottage with a tiled roof, central front door and paned windows either side. The front garden needed a session of weeding but the stone footpath pavers were all in place and the whole dwelling oozed a latent romantic charm. For all its careless unloved demeanour it appeared to have been maintained in a reasonable condition. At least one she could live with.

Quick side glances let her mind tick over with the possibilities. Mow the grass, weed big time, and plant bulbs and loads of flower seedlings to liven and colour it up for spring. A chat with Gran and Ivy Ashford would soon get the garden sorted. They'd probably both love the challenge.

Until she clapped eyes on it, Emma had no idea where her next place in life was meant to be. But her indecision vanished in a heartbeat. This was it. She hadn't even set foot in the place but she just knew.

'Bit neglected,' Emma murmured, stepping along the overgrown path to the front door, trying not to sound too enthusiastic. She didn't even know the price yet. Being an historic property, it could well be exorbitant. Especially in the thriving tourist region around Tingara.

'Reserve your judgement until you've seen inside but I feel you'll be intrigued,' Anne suggested as she unlocked it, the heavy old door releasing a long slow groan of protest as she shoved it open with one shoulder.

The cottage was empty and gloomy in the late afternoon but Anne flicked on all the lights as they went and Emma's eagerness peaked. She even began to visualise how she might furnish it. The open fireplaces in most rooms beckoned with images of cold nights snuggled before them. She suppressed forbidden images of she and Mal in *Clovelly*. The elegant ceiling roses still bore what looked like their original light fittings. Easily replaced, Emma thought, then wondered if they might be restored. It would be fun poking around antique shops. Alone. Again her thoughts flashed to Mal but she shook herself back to reality. She must stop thinking about him but knew it would take time.

Anne remained silent throughout the property tour, leading ahead, her neatly cut auburn hair glowing in the soft lights overhead, looking smart in her fitted suit and sensible chunky heeled shoes.

'I have to say I'm definitely interested,' Emma admitted, opening cupboard doors in the kitchen at the rear of the house which adjoined a cosy dining area and sitting room with bay windows that took advantage of the rear garden and creek view lower down.

She had already decided the kitchen would suit a complete makeover in a cottagey French provincial style. Other than that, the gorgeous old claw bath needed to be resurfaced and she would install a modern shower, but the ambience Emma absorbed from the interior surroundings made her feel that she could make a home here. Even alone.

Being honest with herself, Emma silently

bled. For Mal. And moving on without him. She craved him so much when she should not and missed him with an unbearable ache. He had snuck under her radar and she let herself fall in love. Well, thanks to her poor choice in Steve and track record with men, there was no marriage on the horizon any time soon.

Thinking of her ex, Emma muttered under her breath, 'Bastard!' forgetting who stood alongside.

'Pardon?' Anne stared at her in alarm. 'What did you say?'

Thinking quickly, Emma cleared her throat and said, 'Um . . . *past it*. I was just wondering if this little gem isn't past it.'

She swiftly recovered her poise, pushing her personal difficulties aside. They had no place in deciding her future. Focus Emma.

Anne swiftly turned into agent mode again with a spiel of all the cottage attributes, its location, little to do inside and out. Token efforts to bring the property up to scratch, that sort of thing.

'A lick of paint here and a bit of tinkering there,' she said. 'Cosmetic stuff really. Nothing major.'

Emma agreed but hardly needed convincing. She was already sold. Only one obstacle.

'Please tell me it's cheap.' She folded her hands together as if in prayer and turned a pleading gaze onto her companion.

Anne's pleased smile, presumably at Emma's positive reaction to the cottage, was reassuring but she still cringed. Would it be good news or bad?

'I'm sure there's room to manoeuvre with the owner,' Anne said. 'Surprisingly he's had it on the market for some months with only minor interest. I'm sure he would be approachable to an offer. What's your budget?'

Emma squirmed as she mentioned a figure and her modest deposit available.

'Hmm,' Anne tapped a pen against her clipboard and slipped into negotiation mode. 'Not ten per cent of the asking price but I'm sure we could work something out.'

The agent's interest rose a notch, however, when Emma quickly mentioned the imminent Sydney property sale to support her offer with the knowledge of future forthcoming funds. 'Trouble is,' she said, 'We don't know how long the apartment will take to sell. It might be snapped up or it might not.'

When Emma told Anne the suburb, the agent's eyebrows lifted in awe. 'Darling Point? On the harbour?' she said with a wry grin. 'Not a problem.'

'Well then, pending a structural survey,' Emma said, casting her glance around,

'Although I doubt this solid old place needs it, looks like I've just bought a house.'

The women shook hands on the deal.

'I have all the paperwork for you back at the office.'

'Looks like I'm going to need a handyman,' Emma joked lightly.

She knew one of course and her chest pulled with a tight ache. But good old reliable Will would help. After all, as an architect, he'd designed and built his own unique home. And helped Ginny Bates remodel the old church. He would have suggestions for the best way to approach her minor renovations. Besides, she could always ask the blokes at the local hardware store and there was no reason she couldn't learn some handy girl skills herself.

Emma flipped through the contact list on her mobile phone and made a call as she walked back to Anne's car.

'I've just bought the blacksmith's cottage,' she gushed before Gran barely had a chance to answer. 'But you and Ivy will need to help me with the garden.'

* * *

In the following weeks, as approaching winter pulled a colder wet grip on the countryside with thick frosts and drifts of steady soaking rain, while gusty winds blew the last leaves from trees, Emma threw herself into the work of repairing and furnishing her new home. She still lived with Gran for the moment while the outdated cottage kitchen was ripped out and a new one, including a gleaming Aga range cooker, was installed.

Gran's little car, now repaired and with its owner's permission, saw Emma behind the wheel speeding all over the district chasing *finds* to suit the cottage and nosing out bargains.

When time permitted during the week and some evenings, Emma cleaned the cottage, refreshed the paint on walls where necessary using Will's advice on heritage colours and placed her growing collection of furniture in its rightful place in her new home. Other days, she laboured on creating the growing number of jewellery commissions she received. Despite the raw weather, weekend trade at The Stables could be frantic. Her colourful creative pieces sold hotly, with orders being placed online via her web site and Facebook business page, where she received glowing comments like *trendy* and *unique*.

Amidst it all, Emma tried to stop hurting over Mal and move on. Some days it worked. Others were a flop because she kept tormenting herself over an inability to maintain any lasting relationship. Meanwhile her divorce proceedings from Steve were underway, the papers filed and a court hearing date set. With their Sydney apartment on the market, she kept postponing the necessary trip north to collect the rest of her stuff but knew the trip was inevitable. And soon.

Emma couldn't face walking Mate past *Clovelly* these days so she took a new route along the creek toward her cottage to check on progress and smugly admire its cuteness by gaping from the front gate.

Gran was now recovered from her ordeal and brief hospital stay, commenting casually yet with a certain purpose on the auction sign now in place at *Clovelly*.

'It looks grand now it's finished, especially with the restored garden and the new tree plantings. It seems Mal isn't around any more though.'

It was the first time either of them had mentioned his name in weeks. 'No. I guess he was just here to work on the house. His life is in Bendigo.'

Thankfully, Gran's well known bluntness didn't surface. Her rare tact overcame any further curiosity or questions and she didn't pursue the subject. For which Emma was relieved and grateful. She was finding it hard to remove someone she *truly* loved from her life. But Gran was no fool. Emma knew she watched her false upbeat cheerfulness over her cottage project with suspicion and probably guessed the changed situation in her personal life anyway.

Pushing back her fear, Emma forced herself early one morning on her doggy walk with Mate to swing cautiously by *Clovelly*. In her raincoat with its hood up and secured, water dripping everywhere from its edges, gloved hands sunk deep into her pockets and her boots unable to miss the vast puddles on the pathways, she peered ahead for any sign of Mal's ute. It wasn't there, of course. Not a day passed when he wasn't in her thoughts.

Mate sensed familiar territory and whined at the closed gate. Emma glanced over the freshly painted fence and immaculately tidy house and garden. The landscaper had done wonders with a formal Victorian layout, the central stone fountain she recognised as the one Mal bought on their day out together, and mature plantings. A huge auction sign dominated the front yard now like an advertising hoarding with gorgeous photographs of the restored interior. It looked stunning and announced a date some weeks forward. Emma's heart leapt and she wondered if Mal would return for it. To see the family ancestral home sold. She memorised the date. No harm attending out of curiosity and staying out of sight.

★ ★ ★

Only a matter of days later, Emma received an odd telephone call from Steve that the apartment had been sold and to come up to Sydney to take anything she wanted. Within the week. Possession was something ridiculous like seven days. She thought it strange that he didn't sound more excited.

With the sale he could now pay off his debts. Even if it didn't leave him anything, at least the financial burden no longer hung over his head. He could start over.

Couldn't we all, she thought dismally, knowing she would much rather have Mal in the picture? Instead of brooding over a man she was not fated to have, she turned her thoughts to who could care for Gran while she was away, and packed for a few days in Sydney which she arranged for mid week, planning to return for next weekend's trade again at The Stables.

Will promised to keep an eye on progress at the cottage, and also Gran, who crisply protested that she was perfectly fine and able to take care of herself. Nonetheless, Emma also worded up Muriel next door to pop in each day and when Will arrived to drive her to Albury airport, they left Gran ungraciously muttering about being told what to do.

Emma caught one of many daily short flights to Sydney. To her surprise, in a phone text Steve even offered to pick her up at the airport on arrival. After landing and collecting her bag, Emma waited for almost an hour with still no sign of him. Out of character because he was normally punctual. The capital city traffic gridlock was notorious so maybe he'd been held up. Yet she had received no call or text from him about that or any other reason for the delay.

In the end she decided not to wait, whipped off an SMS to him and grabbed a taxi. Within half an hour she had arrived at the apartment. Stepping from the cab, Emma glanced up at the square cube low rise apartment building, thinking how posh it all looked now with its millionaire residents. Originally this and neighbouring harbour side enclaves were once home to farmers and fisherman. There was only one sleek black car parked in the otherwise deserted street. Emma only noticed because residents hereabouts usually garaged their expensive vehicles. She buzzed the doorbell but, with no answer, used her own key and let herself in.

She dumped her small case in the hallway. 'Steve?'

All was gleaming and silent. The main suite bedroom hadn't been slept in and Steve was nowhere to be found. Perhaps he was caught up on business trying to restore his flagging finances with yet another deal. Emma phoned him again but there was still no answer. She frowned. This was really strange since Steve lived on his phone. There was rarely a time when it wasn't anchored to his ear as he walked or paced his office, or his hands free set up in the car so he was always within reach.

Forgetting Steve's unusual absence for the moment, Emma's gaze swept the apartment. She hadn't realised it was so stark and ultra modern. Sparsely furnished. All glass and black chrome and uncomfortable chairs. After being away for a year, she saw Sydney and what she had previously thought of as her spectacular home here with a whole new perspective. Her return only confirmed that the gloss of her former lifestyle had long since worn off and her home town of Tingara was the place she was meant to be.

She unpacked her few clothes in the guest suite, showered and changed before setting to work rummaging through her crammed walk in wardrobe. She stood back and gaped at it all, hands on hips, shaking her head. How could she possibly have needed all this stuff?

Emma sighed with dismay at the sight of all her expensive clothes glittering on their hangers. How materialistic their life had been. It all seemed so superficial now. What to do with it all? These fancy city clothes were inappropriate for Tingara's op shop but, who knew? Maybe a weekend city visitor would grab a bargain. Emma bundled some of them carelessly into a spare bag and set them aside.

When darkness fell, she found a tin of soup in the half empty pantry, heated it in the microwave and strolled out onto the front patio, standing at the railing spooning it up while admiring the twinkling lights all around the stunning harbour views. The arched bridge, opera house. All gorgeous and soon to be appreciated by new owners. No doubt the reason this prime piece of property had so swiftly sold.

Returning indoors and nursing a mug of tea later reclining on the sumptuous white leather sofa, Emma phoned her married sister, Julie.

'Hey Jules.'

'Em!'

She heard childish squeals in the background. 'Sorry. Forgot you'd be bathing the kids.'

'No drama. Chris has them under control. More or less,' she chuckled.

Emma explained her brief stay and the possibility of catching up. 'Want to come into the city or should I grab a cab out to you?'

Too bad if Steve returned while she was away. It would only take her a few minutes to sign the legal papers anyway which she could do either here or at the lawyers, depending on where they were being held. The main reason for her visit was to gather any meaningful belongings and scoot back to Tingara as soon as possible.

'Lunch please!' Julie laughed. 'I grab any opportunity for brief freedom. Zach will be at school and our folks will have Mia for a few hours. I'll drop her off on the way into town. You going to see them while you're here?'

'Sure.' Emma had hoped a phone call would be adequate. Any personal visit would be short and obligatory but Emma would do her duty. 'Heard from Richard lately?'

Julie chuckled. 'You know our brother. Hardly the communicator.'

'Surely even surfies have mobile phones. I can't believe he's only toying with his medical career to bum about the coast.'

'He's always bunked expectations. He'll settle one day.'

The sisters made the arrangement for just after eleven the following day at a harbour side cafe, giving Emma time to scour through more cupboards in the morning. Surely Steve would return by then. They chatted a while longer until Emma's niece and nephew demanded stories before bed and Julie hung up.

Intuition made Emma pause before she phoned her parents to organise that visit. She would finish packing first, sign the papers when Steve appeared and maybe head out to the family home before she left. She was still niggled with serious annoyance that they had revealed hcr whereabouts to Steve but that was water under the bridge now so she should probably let it go. Except their thoughtless action had triggered her split with Mal and the emotional blow was proving hard to overcome.

Next day, Emma all but finished her apartment sorting so by late morning she dressed for her sisterly lunch outing and strode down to the Darling Point wharf to catch a ferry across the harbour to the city.

Being further north and on the coast, the winter air was so much milder here than icy Tingara but a salty keen breeze blew in off the water. Emma was grateful for the long cardigan she had pulled over her jeans and smart white shirt, finishing her outfit with high heels. It was a year since she had bothered wearing them and almost regretted it as she teetered up the gang plank and on board. She had been aware of someone following close behind as she walked and shouldn't have felt nervous but with Steve missing, Emma had grown uneasy.

It was an invigorating forty minute journey over to the first stop at Garden Island then into circular quay in the city. The trip evoked memories of grander formal nights on extravagant luxury yachts drinking the best wines, eating the best food, often flown in especially from elsewhere, with a fixed smile on her face and rubbing shoulders with Steve's fellow wealthy contacts and some-times dubious friends.

Emma sighed. Those days seemed of another time. As though another person had lived her life instead. It all felt so distant and foreign now.

When the ferry docked, Emma disem-barked and walked around to a nearby waterfront cafe. Stepping into its rustic brick interior, she immediately caught sight of her sister, already at their booked table by a window overlooking the water. She wove between crowded tables toward her. Emma noted with delight a bottle of white wine already chilling in a bucket on their table.

Julie rose and they warmly hugged and kissed.

'You've cut your hair.' Emma smiled.

'Do you like it?'

'Absolutely. You always had natural curls. With the shorter length they've kicked back into life. Cute.'

'Thanks. It's so much easier to manage.'

'Been here long?'

'Ten minutes. Had a good run in with traffic. I thought you'd choose something more posh,' Julie added, looking over their surroundings.

Emma tried not to be offended by her sister's honesty. Their relationship was strong for that very reason and, after all, she spoke the truth.

'I'm done with fancy.'

'Pleased to hear it,' Julie grinned. 'I love this place.'

'Clever of you to suggest meeting early for a leisurely drink before we order lunch,' Emma said as she sat down and let her gaze drift over all manner of water craft messing about on the harbour, sunlight bouncing off its surface.

Julie wrinkled her nose. 'Have to get back

reasonably early before Mia gets restless and difficult for the folks. I had to tell them where I was going. Sorry. Said you'd contact them as soon as you were free.'

'Sure. I'm putting it off but I'll force myself to brave them before I go.'

'Because they blabbed to Steve?'

Emma nodded and clinked glasses with Julie after she poured the wine. 'It had repercussions,' she explained after taking a sip.

'In what way?'

Emma groaned. 'I knew you'd ask.' She paused then plunged ahead. 'I did meet someone.'

Julie's face lit up then shadowed. 'Did? It's over?'

Emma nodded. 'I was dumped. Can't catch a break.'

'Why?'

'Because he saw me kissing Steve and read something into nothing. And then claimed that we got together too fast. And he's ten years younger than me.'

Emma watched for her sister's reaction.

'Really?' She folded her arms on the table and leant forward. 'Name?'

'Mal.'

'Just Mal? He doesn't have a last name?'

'Webster. He lives in Bendigo but he was

182

working on their old family place in Tingara. *Clovelly* out on Wattle Gully Road. Do you remember it?'

'Yes, I do. And?' Julie prompted. 'I feel a question brewing.'

Emma sighed. 'Jules, before you divorce, and if you meet someone else, are you breaking any rules? Should you feel guilty?'

'I'm surprised you even ask. Your marriage was over long before you separated. But my answer to your question is no. If your feelings are dead for Steve and you'd developed new ones for this Mal bloke, then definitely not.' She hesitated, considering her words. 'Em, it's a fact of life that when you take your wedding vow and sign on the dotted line, by law you're married. It never says it will last forever. I'm sorry, Em, but we always knew he was *slick Steve*. I could see you adored him so it was the hardest thing not to blurt out the truth about the man you were about to marry. Everyone else could see but you were blind.'

Emma cast her gaze aside. 'I've learned my lesson and that part of my life is almost over now.'

'I'm starved. Should we order?' Julie interrupted their heavy conversation.

Whether deliberate or not, Emma was grateful. She chose oysters and a salad. Julie preferred a grilled steak.

When the waitress left and Julie topped up their drinks, Emma asked wistfully, 'You're happily married. How *do* you know it's the right one, Jules?'

Her sister shrugged. 'I'm no love guru. In my case, I simply went with my heart. Plus I drilled Chris with a bunch of questions just for good measure,' she smiled. 'Bottom line? It all comes down to some serious chemistry that either exists or doesn't. Age, background and all that stuff has nothing to do with it. You either *connect* or you don't. Outside of that, we've always respected each other. Neither of us takes crap from the other. We're friends, we laugh a lot, we talk a lot. Great sex helps, too, of course.'

'Are you blushing?' Emma teased.

'I hate to see all that loving go to waste. We have Zach and Mia but I'm clucky again. I want another child.'

'What does Chris say?'

'Go for it. Children are the icing on our wedding cake, Em. They're exhausting and challenging and adorable but we'd die for them. So . . . we're trying for another.'

Emma *so* envied her sister's bliss and stability. She could never admit, even to Jules, just how incredibly lonely she felt at times despite her thriving business. She craved Mal

184

with such a deep emptiness she wondered if it would ever ease.

Their food arrived so they settled to eating and quieter conversation for a while.

'I do have *some* good news,' Emma announced. 'My life's not all doom and gloom.'

'Pleased to hear it. Give,' Julie urged.

'I bought a house in Tingara. Well, a cottage really. Small. Two bedrooms but cute and dripping with character. One of the oldest buildings in town. Solid bluestone.'

Julie studied her for a long moment. 'So you're definitely settling in Tingara then?'

Emma nodded. 'It's where I want to be. It feels right. Tingara's a lovely peaceful place. I'd forgotten how much I loved small town life since we left.'

'I do seem to remember you were the only one of us three kids that complained about moving to Sydney all those years ago.'

'I've realised that I need the simplicity of Tingara. It's familiar. I've lived there before. People know me. It's a personal supportive way of life. Now the apartment is sold here in Sydney I can afford the cottage without a mortgage and have something left over.'

'I wonder what Steve's plans are next. I heard on the grapevine that he's on a downhill slide.'

'Pretty much,' Emma confirmed. 'But that's his problem now.'

'So, how is dear old Steve?' Julie asked.

'That's the mystery. I haven't seen him since arriving yesterday.'

'Tactfully avoiding you? Giving you space?'

Emma shook her head and frowned. 'No. He was supposed to meet me at the airport but he didn't show. Frankly, I'm worried.'

'Steve's a survivor. He'll show up eventually.'

'I guess you're right.'

They finished their meal and lingered over a coffee before Julie checked her watch and offered to drive Emma back to the apartment before heading home herself.

As they pulled up on the street and Julie let the car idle, Emma said, 'Say hi to Chris and give the kids a hug from Auntie Em.'

'Will do.'

'Good luck with number three.'

'Thanks.'

'Try to come down south soon, won't you? Zach and Mia should see their great grandmother,' Emma hinted.

'Promise.'

They hugged and parted, Emma watching her sister drive away until the vehicle was out of sight. The same shiny black car was parked further up the street she noticed as she checked the apartment mailbox and flipped through the envelopes. Mostly windows and bills by the look of it. But one was unstamped and must have been hand delivered. It simply said *To the householder*. Maybe it was one of those bulk advertising mail outs.

Back up in the apartment, she was about to bin it after tossing the others onto the granite kitchen counter top. But instinct and curiosity made her open it. When she did and read the few short handwritten words, Emma froze in shock.

We're watching you.

Clearly it was a warning and meant for Steve.

Alone in the apartment and with her estranged husband mysteriously absent, Emma shivered and hurried around to check all the doors and windows were locked. It was still Wednesday and she was virtually finished sorting her stuff. Her return flight was booked for Friday but a bad feeling rolled through her stomach and she considered leaving a day earlier, tomorrow. Steve or the lawyers could mail her the documents to sign, surely.

For the rest of the afternoon and night, Emma jumped nervously at every sound, feeling threatened just by being in the apartment. Being without a car left her utterly defenceless. She was contemplating the worst and the most dire scenario but after a sleepless night, Thursday morning came, the sun rose and all was well.

Emma laughed at her own paranoid alarm.

9

The day Mal Webster watched Emma walk away from *Clovelly* his heart squeezed with pain and his world crumbled. Changed forever. Breaking up with her rated as the dumbest thing he'd ever done. Worse than the other time in his life when he'd really stuffed up because he was older and wiser now. He should have handled the situation a thousand times better. His own double standard gnawed at him every single day. Too much damn thinking. He grew mad at himself.

So he pushed himself hard and worked day and night with little sleep to finish *Clovelly* within a week. He ignored his business back in Bendigo, leaving it idle along with only a skeleton crew, a handful of loyal guys he'd probably have to let go anyway.

The sooner he cut ties with Tingara the better for everyone. The landscapers would finish work in the garden but as he turned the big old key to lock the front door, he loped down the broad stone steps to stand back and admire his work. Pride swelled in his chest but not enough to ease the heavier burden of his own making.

Feet apart and hands on hips, he knew it was time to move on. This part of his life and family heritage was over. Like any future with Emma. But where to now? He had obligations and family in Bendigo, reasons to return, but his future stretched out ahead kind of bleak and it had nothing to do with the oncoming winter.

He pulled up his coat collar, braced himself against the cutting wind and strode for the ute, with vague thoughts as he drove away that he might swing back to Tingara for the *Clovelly* auction in a few weeks. And told himself he would return for no other reason than that.

He and Will were working on their exciting new housing project together which meant returning to Tingara from time to time. He hoped he did and didn't run into Emma again. It would kill him to see that beautiful face, that long wavy hair swinging around her shoulders knowing he couldn't touch. He had let himself fall in love while she belonged to another man. An older man, her own age.

So the guy was down on his luck but so was Mal. His business was struggling and it could be years before he and Will saw any financial rewards from their project, if at all. They would either make or lose a shed load of money.

All things considered, his life and finances were both on shaky ground these days. All for the best that he and Emma were no longer involved. What did he have to offer her right now anyway?

Through all of the weeks since they parted, Mal was wracked with guilt that he had a secret of his own. His past wasn't squeaky clean either. He'd been working around to telling Emma when he'd seen her with Steve. That moment soured his gut because, until then, he had come to thinking Emma was his. In every way. He saw a future. Hope. Love.

Then it had all been dashed and gone belly up when her words floated across the street and hit him. She hadn't loved the guy when she'd married him. It had rocked him because he'd been giving serious thought to them as a couple.

After that, it took a lot of convincing himself that he'd done the right thing in splitting with Emma. Who was he kidding? He had questioned his hasty decision ever since. Hell, he'd only made it out of jealousy anyway, seeing her with another man. Hating her husband's arms around her and leaping to wrong conclusions. He knew the woman better than that and he'd done her a great injustice by his reaction.

As the weeks passed, in the middle of the

night, Mal had taken to nursing a drink and pacing. Not his usual style but he was plagued with regret. He decided on doing something crazy. It could only backfire and he sure had nothing to lose.

So one Thursday morning, Mal stopped off at his business office, handed out a few instructions and told the guys he would be away overnight.

When Mary opened the door of her Tingara flat, Mal unclenched his fists. Emma always answered if she was home. This was good. He could get a heads up from Mary before he faced Emma.

'Malcolm Webster.' She beamed. 'This is such a pleasure. I've missed you.' She stepped forward and placed her tiny arms around his waist in a hug.

Once ushered warmly inside, Mal felt like he was coming home. He'd never been close to his parents. His only sibling and brother, Alex, was off exploring the world so it was good to have a sense of family of sorts, if only by association. He had nowhere else he could go in Tingara now *Clovelly* was done, except maybe to bunk on Will Bennett's lumpy sofa.

Mal glanced around the living room like he expected it had changed in a few weeks. Mary's knick knacks were still crammed and dusty in glass cabinets and on shelves. His heart beat faster knowing he was in Emma's territory and she could walk in that door any minute.

How would they both react? What would they do or say? On his own part he'd like to blurt out *I'm sorry. I want you back.*

He sauntered into the kitchen, hands in his pockets, feeling lost.

Mary smiled as he entered. 'Sit down. Jug's boiled. I'm making a cuppa and have a fresh batch of scones Will dropped off from the bakery.'

As Mal managed to fit his long legs under the small round table, Mary brought over a plate of scones thick with butter and raspberry jam before him.

'You like it strong and black, right?' She set down a large mug of tea.

He nodded. 'Thanks Mary. It's good to see you again.'

'I expect you're hoping to see someone else, too?' she grinned, bringing over her own flowery tea cup and saucer to join him.

'Not sure I'd know what to do if I did,' he admitted.

'Emma's in Sydney at the moment with Steve,' she said gently. Mal's chest tightened at the hasty thought of them possibly getting back together until Mary continued, 'She has stuff to sort out, you know. The apartment sold quickly so she's packing up. Probably have the divorce to discuss, too.' Gran slipped him a cheeky glance. 'I'm sure you still have her mobile number?'

'As it happens, I do,' he drawled.

'Couldn't hurt to phone her and have a chat, could it?'

Mal squirmed. 'She'll be busy. Maybe I should wait till she gets back.'

'Why waste time?' Mary challenged. 'Don't get to my age and have regrets.'

Mal chuckled and his mood lightened. 'Mary Hamilton you're sneaky. But amazing.'

He finished another scone and lingered a while before taking his leave.

She whispered, 'Good luck,' as he walked away.

Mal drove to a quiet place on the edge of town, pulled over in the ute to send Emma a text and waited because he was too much of a coward to call and speak to her in person until he knew her response. Easy steps, he thought, but he needed to get this guilt off his chest. He needed Emma to know. He owed her that at least.

* * *

When the phone rang in the quiet Darling Point apartment, Emma jumped in fright. At last. Finally Steve had bothered to call. She raced to it and snatched it up.

'Missing your husband, Emma?'

She swallowed against her surprise. Not Steve but she knew that threatening voice, she just couldn't place it right now. This had everything to do with Steve's money troubles. And why he was missing. Her faith was indifferent at the best of times but she silently crossed her fingers and prayed he was okay. Was this one of his creditors? A business associate? What were they up to?

Emma played it cool and said, 'Not particularly. He'll soon be my ex and he's probably with another woman anyway.'

She recognised Steve's laugh in the background and realised she must be on speaker phone at the other end for him to have heard her comment. She hadn't realised she was holding her breath and tense until she relaxed and let her fear escape. Steve was alive. But goodness knows where.

'What do you want?' she snapped, covering her distress with bravado.

'We're entertaining your husband as our house guest. For collateral you understand. Don't do anything stupid. The apartment is bugged and we've tapped your mobile phone. Keep it handy. We'll be in touch.' The line went dead.

Emma's hand shook as she hung up. Steve had danced with the wrong devil this time. She just wished she could remember the voice so she knew which one.

Her heart thumped with dread as she stumbled into the kitchen and poured a glass of wine from the half empty bottle she had started last night. Her mind raced with thoughts. How did they get into the apartment? Steve's own key? It could only have been while she was out yesterday for a few hours when she met Julie for lunch in the city. How did they know her movements? She was obviously being watched but how? From where?

Then it hit her. The black car on the street. She strode outside. With a hand up to shade her eyes against the bright winter sun, she saw it was still there. Parked three house blocks down. She marched toward it but its engine fired up and the vehicle sped away. With tinted windows, it had been impossible to see inside. Besides, she was hardly close enough anyway. But not so far away that she didn't catch the number plate. She repeated it like a mantra as she raced back into the apartment to write it down. She had no idea what she could do with it but it was a start. A small piece of evidence to trace whoever was holding Steve.

Emma recalled at one of the many parties she and Steve threw, a techie friend had hacked into their wireless security system because he could and just for fun, witnessing everything inside the apartment from his device. These thugs who had Steve might just have done the same thing and she wasn't taking any chances. No one was perving on her. She must disable it. Just in case. Ideas were already brewing in her mind and she didn't plan on being seen when she put them into action.

She strode into Steve's orderly office and went straight to his filing cabinet. He was meticulous with paperwork so she easily found the installation book for their security system. She could shut it down but the battery backup would kick into action so she needed to disconnect that, too. Her finger trembled as she scrolled through the contents to find the page she needed. She flipped to it, swiftly read the instructions, memorised it and set to work.

Armed with a pair of pliers, first she went to the main switchboard and turned off the power then to the security control panel box in the utility cupboard. She unlocked it, disconnected the red and black battery backup leads, cut the wires to the circuit board and locked it again.

When Emma returned to the living room and her mobile phone beeped with a message, she presumed it would be Steve's *hosts*. It wasn't.

She plumped down onto the sofa in shock. If ever she needed a friend it was now. Mal had contacted her! She could have cried with joy and astonishment to read his words.

Thinking of you. Can I call you?

But no way could she talk on this phone. She needed somewhere untraceable outside the apartment. She seized on an idea and sent back a text.

Please don't. I'll be in touch.

$\star$ $\star$ $\star$

It plagued Emma knowing she should go to the police. She had a vehicle number plate. That should give them a start with their investigations surely. If only she could remember that voice. But they had given her a subtle warning against it so, for now, she would do as they said until she saw how this all played out.

She escaped the apartment by the downstairs back entrance that overlooked the water and scrambled through bushes between neighbouring property gardens until she reached the end of the street where it turned into a narrow lane.

Feeling absolutely ridiculous skulking around a posh suburb, Emma worked her way along back streets she knew two blocks across from the apartment building. They led to a public telephone box opposite the nearby village store and cafe.

Emma fed coins into the slot and felt a deep warmth of reassurance flood through her at the sound of Mal's voice when he answered.

'Did I interrupt something before?' he asked.

'No,' she gasped, 'I can't call from the apartment.'

'Can't?' There was a pause and his tone immediately grew concerned. 'Are you okay? You sound out of breath.'

'I've been running. Didn't realise I was so unfit. Walking Mate is a piece of cake by comparison.' She closed her eyes, took a calming breath and began to explain. 'I need you to do exactly as I ask please.'

It was as if they had never disagreed and been apart. Emma confided everything and her current dicey situation at the apartment.

'Honey, if I leave now I can be there in six hours.'

'Mal, no!'

'We'll need wheels,' he said as if he hadn't

heard her plea, 'I need to be there with you.'

'There's nothing you can do.'

'I can at least be there.'

'Mal,' she paused, 'You have to know that I want nothing more than to see you again but not like this in these circumstances. It's not your responsibility.'

'It's not yours either,' was his comeback.

'This is serious stuff. I just have to see how it plays out. I've been warned but I don't feel under threat. They just want their money and they're holding Steve until they get it. I don't want you dragged into this.' Mal let out a sharp sigh at the other end. Emma gripped the phone tighter. 'It's so good to hear your voice,' she said softly. 'It's like ESP that you contacted me now.'

'You said you're in a public phone box. Call the police. Tell them everything you just told me and don't go back to the apartment. At least you'll be safe.'

'Mal, I can't let Steve down and put him in jeopardy if they find out I disobeyed their orders. I know this is all his doing and I may not have truly loved him in the full romantic sense.' There, she had voiced the underlying issue between them. 'But I'm not so heartless that I don't care about him as a human being. We were together five years, Mal. That counts for something. I at least owe him loyalty until this dodgy business is done.'

'Damn it, Emma, your life's at stake here. Don't you get that?'

'Yes and I appreciate your frustration and concern but I've made my decision. I'll stay here in the apartment for two days until the money goes through and Steve's released.'

'You don't know who you're dealing with or if that will even happen.'

'It's hard to explain but I have a gut feeling about all this. I think he'll be okay. Maybe they thought Steve would do a runner but for whatever reason they're holding him, I don't feel a sense of danger. Just threats.'

Emma knew her certainty had something to do with the mystery voice and she frowned, still unable to remember.

She heard Mal's deep sigh. 'Okay. We'll play by your rules but I'm still driving up.'

'If you insist.' Emma smiled into the phone. There wasn't much either of them could do for now but she loved his take-charge attitude. Made her feel less like she was struggling alone. 'You won't be able to contact me until you arrive so just text me something like *Hi Emma* when you arrive and I'll meet you at this phone box.' She explained its location.

'I'm leaving now so I'll see you in about six hours. Take care,' he ended softly.

Emma returned to the apartment and anxiously watched the clock slowly tick away time. She ate, watched television, made endless coffee, read a bit, paced a lot, her mobile phone always at her side. There was no further contact from Steve's bully, whoever he was.

As afternoon became evening, Emma wandered out onto the terrace. At this time of day its direct view of the orange streaked sunset shone from behind the iconic arch of the harbour bridge.

Mal was late. Even as she thought it, her mobile beeped from the living room behind her. She dashed to check it. *Hi Emma*. She grinned. He was here.

★   ★   ★

Leaving the lights on in the apartment so her minders would assume she was in, Emma left to meet Mal. It proved tricky finding her way through the back streets again in the dusk of evening but she couldn't wait to see her man again. Any hiatus between them seemed of far less concern than her present predicament.

She recognised his parked ute half a block away. He opened the door, stepped out and stretched. Neither spoke. He looked weary and adorable and when she fell into his arms, it felt like coming home.

'It's so good to see you,' she whispered. He kissed her forehead and hugged her tighter. 'I can't believe you came all this way.'

'I'd die for you,' he murmured.

Emma gasped. Until then, she had held herself together. Now, tears pooled in her eyes. When she looked up at him, Mal kissed them away.

'I booked into a motel nearby. Can you get away for a while?'

She nodded. 'But not for long. They're likely to phone any time.'

'What happens if you don't answer?'

'Frankly I don't care but I'll just tell them I was in the shower or sleeping, whatever. They can believe me or not.'

Mal led her to the ute, opened her door and Emma sank into the vehicle's familiar comfort.

Once inside the motel, Mal dumped his bag and she asked, 'How long can you stay?'

'As long as you need me.'

She grinned, crossed her fingers and took a chance. 'What if that's forever?'

His eyes lit up but there was a reserved wariness behind them. 'Then I guess I'll stick around. If you'll have me.'

'Why wouldn't I?'

He shrugged and ran a hand through his

thick hair. 'I need to speak to you about something and that might make a difference.'

'Oh?' Emma wondered what was coming next. He looked more than serious. *Afraid* was the word she would use to describe the look on his face.

He ran his hand over it and said, 'I want to apologise for how I treated you back in Tingara. Sending you away like a cold bastard as though I didn't care.'

'You explained your reasons.'

Emma was trying to be charitable because Mal was talking to her, reaching out and for that alone, she was comforted and grateful. Her heart ached with love to see him again but she sensed now wasn't the time to laugh with him and love him and touch him which she had previously taken for granted. Right now, he clearly had something else on his mind.

'I was jealous and judged you too harshly. Plus I wasn't completely honest with you or myself. You had the courage to be upfront about not marrying Steve for love. My past isn't unblemished either.'

'I guess we all have skeletons.' Emma shrugged, being generous but filled with unease about what Mal might tell her. 'Things we don't want people to know. For whatever reason. Guilt or shame.'

'Exactly. I blamed you for a lapse of judgement but I've had one of my own. Big time.'

'From what I've seen, I don't believe you're a bad person, Mal,' Emma said, meaning it, and praying his news did not prove insurmountable for them.

'You may not still think so after I explain.'

It seemed important to him that he should tell her so when Mal motioned for her to do so, he paced while Emma sat on the bed and listened.

'I left school at sixteen. All I'd ever wanted to do was work with my hands so I became a builder's apprentice. The parents weren't too happy about it but at least it was a job, even if it didn't pay much. Weekends were for fun and, in those days, drinking. When I was eighteen and had my licence, I bought my first ute and went out socialising hard on Saturday nights, often stupidly ended up drunk. I'd never done a one-night-stand before. Hadn't had much experience with girls up till then but I locked eyes with this girl, Brittany. She was hot.' He shrugged. 'You can guess what happened.'

His searching glance at Emma told her he was gauging her reaction. So far it all seemed like a teenage indiscretion but she let him continue.

'A few months later, Brittany contacted me and said she was pregnant. I was ashamed of myself actually for not taking responsibility and precautions. Inexperience. I learned my lesson. I met her parents and told them that if I was the father, I would support her financially and in every other way as much as I could. I would never abandon my kid. They're good people and accepted that. After our son, Daniel, was born, and DNA tests proved positive, I grew up fast. I was a father at nineteen and although the circumstances weren't ideal, I loved it. When I finished my apprenticeship, I started my own business, worked hard and built a thriving business until Pete almost ruined me recently.'

Emma's thoughts were only that this experience in Mal's life was probably why he seemed so much more mature for his age. He was a dad by nineteen who'd had responsibility thrust on him yet embraced the challenge. More than some teenage boys might have done, turning their back and walking away.

'You made a mistake but did an honourable thing.' She frowned. 'And sounds like you have a beautiful son in your life as a result. If you're concerned, I don't hate or blame you for what happened.'

'After you explained about not loving Steve and being drawn by his wealth, I judged you on that alone even though I knew you to be different. I started feeling guilty that I'd made myself out to be some kind of better human being. I'm not. I wanted to apologise for that.'

Emma considered what Mal had just confided and could only respect him for his honesty. 'I accept. Thank you for explaining.' She hesitated. 'So what's your situation now with Daniel's mother?'

Mal shrugged. 'There's nothing between us romantically if that's what you mean. I try to be there for her. Babysit when she wants a night out. I have Daniel some Sundays and weekends. Whenever he asks to see me or come visit. He's my little champ. Part of my life now.' His mouth tugged into a half smile of pride. 'I don't have a long line of women in my life these days,' he added quietly, sending her a telling glance.

'So you've discovered I'm not perfect and vice versa. Where do we go from here?' There was a history between them and Emma longed to know.

'I don't know but I hope it's together. I miss *us*.' He hovered nearby, charmingly uncertain.

Emma nodded. 'Me too.'

He took a hesitant step closer.

'We need to get rid of this tension, don't you think?' Emma growled.

'You're so much older and wiser than me,' he teased. 'I was hoping you'd catch on.'

'No wise cracks about my age.'

Amid laughs and kisses they fell back onto the bed. Their clothes disappeared, leaving an untidy trail about the room.

Later, draped across her lover, Emma asked, 'So, what happens now?'

Mal stroked her hair, picked up their soft silky strands and let them slide through his fingers. 'I told you about Daniel on the chance you'd still have me and so you knew what you're getting into if you took me on. We're a team me and my son. A package deal. How do you feel about that?'

'I'm perfectly fine with it and I'd love to meet him.' Emma had one main concern. 'But what if he doesn't like me?'

'Impossible. I love you.' He kissed her nose. 'Daniel will too.'

'Well I'm almost a divorced woman and I've just bought a cottage in Tingara. What do you think of that?'

Mal chuckled and his dimple came into play again. He was so cute. She just bet Daniel would be, too.

'Hope you invite me around to see it.'

'As soon as we get back?'

'Sounds good to me.'

'It's undergoing minor renovations.'

'Ah, so it's a fixer-upper. I'm guessing you need a handyman then?'

'Oh I think I've already found one,' she whispered.

'Now don't make me jealous again or we'll have to do more making up.' Mal rolled over on top of her again, kissing her long and lusciously on her mouth and breasts.

Emma chuckled and, for a while, forgot what else was happening in her life right now. But at a rather exciting moment in the middle of making love, she exclaimed, 'Oh my goodness!'

'That good, huh?' Mal murmured.

'No! That's it!' She playfully smacked his gorgeous bare chest. 'Edward Stenner! The voice on the phone is Teddy.'

Emma knelt on the bed beside him. 'Of course.' She tapped her hand beneath her chin. 'Steve's up to here in debt to him. He'll want his money first. And revenge.'

'What made you remember?'

Emma blushed and put a hand to each warm cheek. 'Actually it happened just before I left Steve. We threw a party and when I went upstairs to our ensuite bathroom, I opened the bedroom door to find a very naked and busty stunning brunette in bed with Teddy.'

Emma caught his unimpressed glance. 'I

know. Nice types, huh? I don't know how he managed it at such short notice but before he left the party that night, Teddy presented me with a beautiful boxed string of perfect pearls. Said it was a thank you gift for a great party but the look he gave me meant it was like silence money. I felt sick.'

She shrugged. 'When I left Steve and Sydney, I guess Teddy figured he was safe and that his glamorous wife would never know.' She rubbed her hands together. 'What makes this so much juicier is the fact that Steve told me he tried to have an affair with Teddy's wife Vivienne to get information. He failed of course. Vivienne led him on then blabbed to Ted. No one crosses the Stenners. Now, there's one strong woman. You don't mess with Vivienne.'

Emma shook her finger at Mal for emphasis. 'And that's why Teddy is taking retribution on Steve now. To settle the score. But I wonder just how Vivienne would react if she knew Teddy had been unfaithful to *her*? She's the power behind that marriage. Fiercely jealous and protective of Teddy. It's well known she rules him with an iron fist.'

Emma chuckled. 'Oh this is too easy and going to be so much fun.' She sighed. 'Of course it won't work if she already knows. I hope she doesn't otherwise I won't have any bargaining power against her.'

After that, as much as Emma adored Mal, she couldn't concentrate. She was too excited with the prospect of what she had in mind, a plan for a little mutual blackmail. So Mal reluctantly drove her to a street near the apartment but out of sight of the black surveillance car so Emma could prepare to put it into action tomorrow. She needed to act fast because settlement for the apartment sale was in two days. Hopefully the monies would be transferred as planned, Steve's funds to Stenner, and Emma's into her personal account. But at this stage Steve's safety was paramount and Emma wanted to introduce some collateral of her own.

10

With a combination of Mal's delicious lovemaking fresh in her mind and the thought of the exhilarating day ahead, Emma barely slept. She only hoped her plan worked.

After being scarcely able to eat anything for breakfast, she dressed carefully. Thank goodness for the last of the designer outfits destined for charity but still hanging in her vast apartment closet. The styles by any socialite standards were a year old and therefore so last season but they were all classics and Emma hoped she could carry it off.

Knowing Vivienne Stenner, Emma chose her apparel carefully. The woman loved pearls so draping a string around her neck was a no brainer. But what to go with it? She needed to project confidence. A suit was too conventional. Something soft yet assured. And it went without saying that heels were a must. Emma sighed.

In the end she chose a neutral coloured figure-hugging trendy dress with a draped neck, the pearls, her polished shoes, long brown hair down and well brushed, topping it off with a splash of glossy chestnut lipstick. She pushed on a giant showy pair of sunglasses, purely for effect, and considered herself good to go.

She walked out the back of the apartment along the water again to meet Mal around the corner. He leant against the ute, arms and legs crossed, watching for her approach. This beautiful young man with his dark good looks flipped her heart yet again in his country casual jeans, white shirt and leather boots.

She spread her arms and turned a circle. 'Do I look the part?'

Mal pushed himself away from the ute, straightened and let out a long soft whistle. 'Stunning? And all this belongs to me?' he drawled.

'Every single centimetre. Let's dare that black car in my street and drive right past it.'

Mal chuckled. 'Living dangerously today, aren't we?'

With Emma's directions, he parked in front of the beauty salon where, without fail, the elegant Vivienne had a weekly standing appointment.

'Wish me luck,' Emma said.

'Go get her gorgeous,' Mal grinned.

Emma strolled into the salon as though she owned it and scanned its dim interior. She lowered her sunglasses to look over the top until her gaze settled on her target at the far end. As she walked toward her, Vivienne's radar kicked in and she flicked up her glance to spy Emma. Recognition was swift when their eyes met.

In that moment, Emma knew she had guessed right. If the Stenners weren't involved in Steve's absence, Vivienne would have smiled warmly and greeted her as she did everyone — with gushing pleasure. Instead, a look of defensive alarm crossed her face. So Emma proceeded with full confidence.

Emma actually admired the woman. Not a wrinkle in sight, platinum hair perfectly groomed, French nails done and a model figure. Although she was willing to bet the woman's boobs were enhanced.

Emma stood over her, secure in her advantage. Besides, she matched this woman for style today and knew it. 'Vivienne.'

'Emma Greenberg.'

'Hamilton. I use my maiden name now.'

Despite her outward assurance, Emma still hoped her instincts were right. Vivienne must know why she was here. She almost expected her to ask *How did you escape the apartment?*

'I know,' Emma said wryly. 'I should be under surveillance, right? But we drove right past your goons and they didn't follow. I guess they expect I'm still obediently inside the apartment.'

'You've changed,' Vivienne accused crisply.

'I've learned.' Emma stared her down. If the other woman wouldn't play nice, neither would she. She wrinkled her nose and beamed. 'Shall we take our conversation private?'

Vivienne pulled her hands from the beautician's ministrations, rose and strode to the front desk. 'Simone, I'll be using your office and I don't want to be disturbed.'

'Of course, Mrs. Stenner.'

'Follow me,' Vivienne hissed as she passed, her heels tapping on the shiny tiled floor.

In the rear office, Vivienne flung open the door, entered and whirled around to face Emma. 'What's this all about?'

Emma quietly closed it behind them. 'You know exactly why I'm here. Like I said, I've learned many things. Especially recently. And before you get any ideas, I have back up. My body guard is outside waiting for me. Just so you know.' She flashed a quick smile. 'Now let's get down to business. You're holding Steve.' Vivienne's eyebrows flickered up but she remained silent. 'Obviously I don't know where. It's called kidnapping and I could go to the police. But if you cooperate we can all leave satisfied with no harm done and no questions asked.'

'Going missing is not a crime.'

'It is if I have serious concerns for the safety and welfare of the person involved.'

'I have no idea what you're talking about but do go on.' Vivienne aimed for bored sophistication but Emma could see she had shaken the woman out of her usual comfort zone of superiority.

'Don't play games with me. I have a life to live and I want to get back to it. So here's the thing. We both know what's happening and why. You want your money.' Emma shrugged. 'Fair enough but there's no need for strong arm tactics. We're talking about ordinary Steve Greenberg here not some gun toting, drug smuggling criminal. Steve made bad business decisions and failed. We've sold the apartment, you'll get your money, so back off.

'It took me a while to recognise your husband's voice on the phone,' Emma continued, 'But Edward,' she used his full name because Vivienne always did and Emma knew she would appreciate the small gesture of respect, 'Has Steve, and I want him released. Now.' When Vivienne started to protest, Emma raised a hand. 'Let me finish. If you don't, I *will* go to the police.'

Vivienne blanched. 'You have no proof.'

'Oh but I do. Steve's paranoid about organisation.' She frowned and gave a short laugh. 'I'm surprised he failed in business really when he's so anal about small things. Like recording every phone call in and out of the apartment. So I'm afraid we have your husband's voice and threatening conversation with me on tape.'

'You're bluffing.'

'You think? I also have what I believe is called leverage. My own personal eye witness proof of Edward's *indiscretion.*'

'How dare you try to blacken his name and reputation,' Vivienne snapped.

'I dare because I saw it myself. Would you care for the exact date and the sordid details?'

'I don't like what you're insinuating.'

'No, I don't suppose you do.' Emma shook her finger. 'But there will be no lies here today, Vivienne. At least, not from me. Only the truth. You may not like or believe it but, trust me, Edward *has* strayed. Probably more than once.' She paused. 'Felicity Wainwright. Our last party at the apartment before I left Steve and Sydney.'

Emma left that nugget of truth sink in then rattled off the date. Easy enough to remember because she left for Tingara the next day. The first day of her year's separation from Steve which was only recently entered on their divorce papers and was still fresh in her mind.

'Feel free to challenge Edward on it. Oh, and you may wish to return these to him. Edward's parting gift to me that same night.'

Emma removed the string of pearls she wore and laid them carefully on the desk, thinking it ironic to give them to the woman who should have rightly received them in the first place. Any similar sumptuous natural pearl necklace would take years to assemble to be exquisitely matched and was usually finished with a similar diamond clasp. She then withdrew a long blue velvet box from her handbag that Vivienne immediately recognised.

'The jeweller's name is inside, as you know, and you also know they keep records of all transactions for their wealthy and exclusive clientele. Date, price, who bought them. It will be one of your employees no doubt, acting on Edward's instructions since your husband made sure he didn't leave the party.'

Vivienne's previous disdain turned into carefully controlled mounting fury. And it wasn't aimed at Emma.

'I know you're keen to chat to your husband. Do give him my regards and tell him I expect Steve back at the apartment, well, pretty much within the hour really, so

I'll leave you to get cracking on it.' As Emma opened the office door, she said, 'I'm off to have a champagne lunch with my lover now. I expect Steve to be at the apartment when I return.'

Emma didn't hear Vivienne move as she walked away, not even to scrape up the incriminating string of pearls that lay between them on the desk.

⋆   ⋆   ⋆

Shaken from her encounter with Vivienne, Emma climbed back into the ute beside Mal.

'You're trembling.' He took her hands in his own and just held them. 'Should I ask how it went?'

'Awesome. I think she bought it. Now I just have to wait and see if my demand to return Steve bears a result.'

'Where to now, then?'

'Can we wait just a minute? I want to see if — ' Emma broke off. 'That was quick.'

Vivienne emerged from the beauty salon as a black limousine slid up to the kerb. She disappeared inside and it sped away.

Emma gasped and grinned. 'Bingo! Okay, now we can do lunch. Any suggestions?'

'Fish and chips on the beach?'

Emma chuckled. 'Not much beach around

here but there's a yacht club nearby right on the water. Too fancy?'

'Honey, it's your day,' he drawled. 'I'll drive. You navigate.'

Ten minutes later saw them walking onto the alfresco deck dining area at the club, nestled on the beautiful foreshore. They chose one of the umbrella-covered tables, gave their drinks order and settled back to appreciate the direct views onto the blue waters of the floating marina and further out across Rushcutters Bay.

As they clinked glasses of celebratory champagne, Emma's brow wrinkled. 'I hope we're not being premature.'

'Judging by Vivienne's hasty departure from the salon, I doubt it. Here's to a positive outcome.'

'I'll second that,' Emma said as they touched glasses.

Mal's wish for fish and chips came true although he would have preferred eating them hot and salty out of white paper instead of in such smart surroundings. But Emma was as much at home and comfortable in this setting as back in small town Tingara. She deserved this moment of triumph. She'd gone out and won it herself. He kept his own counsel though as to whether Steve Greenberg was worth her risk. But full points for her humanity and loyalty to the guy in this whole sorry mess. Mal didn't much like what he saw of the man in Tingara and wondered what his opinion would be up close.

Dressed to kill, Emma caught the eye of most men who passed. Mal no longer buckled with jealousy. Instead, he glowed with a deep sense of love and pride and belonging for his woman, confident now that she genuinely returned his affections.

Despite the glorious setting alongside the woman he loved, Mal sensed Emma's restlessness during lunch. An hour had passed since their arrival, she had hardly touched her meal and he knew her thoughts were elsewhere.

So he suggested, 'Maybe we should head back to the apartment?'

Emma instantly rose to her feet. 'Let's.'

'What if he's not there?' she said as they pulled up outside ten minutes later, no sign of the black mystery car in sight anywhere up or down the street.

Good sign or bad, she wondered?

Back inside, Emma paced for another thirty long minutes, anxious her morning's efforts had all been in vain. Until the key rattled in the lock and Steve breezed through the door.

He and Emma stood and stared at each

other for a long loaded moment. From a side glance, Mal saw her eyes briefly shut and her shoulders relax.

'I hear you were responsible for letting me go early,' Steve said.

'They had no right to hold you against your will.'

Steve scoffed. 'Those people don't play by any rules. At least my stay was in luxury,' he smirked. He oozed a brash confidence now he was free.

No *Thank you, Emma,* she noted and fumed. Steve was infuriatingly unbelievable. Maybe she should have left him where he was.

'Well, I've done my last duty for you,' she said.

'Yeah, you always were good at doing the right thing.'

Emma bristled with unconcealed fury.

Steve's gaze angled behind her, drawn to the man bringing up the rear. 'Who are you? Emma's latest?'

'I'm the man so close to being Emma's fiancé, it's dangerous.' Mal reached out and extended a hand. 'Malcolm Webster.'

Emma gaped dreamily at her man. He wanted to marry her?

Steve rudely stepped around them. 'You're welcome to her. I'm out of here. I'm leaving for the Gold Coast.'

Notorious for slick schemes and money makers. 'Sounds perfect for you. All those suntanned beach babes.' She hesitated but figured she had nothing to lose although she was probably wasting her breath. 'I pulled out all the stops for you today.'

He dragged a slow gaze over her from head to toe. 'So I see. You shouldn't have bothered. They would have released me tomorrow anyway.'

Emma wanted to scream and slap his face. Instead, she hooked a finger in a belt loop of Mal's jeans and playfully tugged him closer. He didn't resist and slid an arm around her waist.

'Then I wish you all the bad luck in the world. I'm leaving with my lover now,' she flung at Steve, hiding her crushing hurt, ashamed that she had ever been associated with this man let alone married to him.

Steve cackled and disappeared upstairs.

'I should never have bothered,' Emma hissed as Mal closed the apartment door behind them for the last time.

'You did what you needed to do in your heart, honey. The mark of an honourable,' he leaned closer, 'And very beautiful woman.'

'You're biased. Do you mind if I stay in the motel with you tonight until the apartment settlement money goes through tomorrow?'

Of course he didn't and vigorously shook his head. He could only fantasize about the awesome night ahead and, later, they took full advantage of the situation.

* * *

Emma cancelled her return flight to Albury since it was a given she would drive back home to Tingara with Mal. After coming all the way up to Sydney and being her support in recent days, not to mention their own personal reunion and the revelation about his son, Daniel, she was quite simply sold on Mal Webster. His high moral life standards and his unbelievable loving only ticked off more boxes.

Early next morning found them packed up, skipping breakfast and edging out through Sydney's notorious traffic, even travelling against the commuter rush after having confirmed Emma's half of the apartment sale was safely transferred into her personal bank account.

Her mood matched the typical start of winter rainy drizzle. She felt in a slump after being caught up and dragged into the upheaval and extraordinary events of recent days. As though she had become a different person than when she left Tingara for Sydney. Had it only been Tuesday?

As the windscreen wipers slapped and the central city became crowded suburbs, Emma phoned her sister, Julie.

'Where are you?'

'On the way to Mum and Dads.' Mal had considerately agreed to meet them.

'Oh but that means you're so close. Do you have time to stop here for a quick coffee? Please?'

Julie sounded so ecstatic, probably to grab a glimpse of Mal. Because Julie was on speaker phone and he heard the conversation, Emma glanced across at him and shrugged her shoulders.

Mal chuckled. 'Why not?'

'Okay. Twenty minutes.' Emma hung up and keyed their changed destination into the GPS. 'You realise my sister has no interest in seeing me again? It's all about you.'

He reached out and squeezed her hand. 'Actually I like the idea of getting involved with your family. Apart from Daniel I don't have much of one myself. Alex rarely comes back to Australia and my parents have backed out of my life since I became an unmarried father.'

'What do they think of Daniel?'

'They haven't really accepted him. Not

interested to see him. When they do they're polite but hands off. They disapprove of his mother, Brittany, but forget I'm equally to blame by not taking my own share of responsibility at the time.' He shrugged. 'Maybe they believe it reflects on them poorly and they share a sense of guilt. I'll never know. They refuse to talk about it.'

Emma glanced across at Mal, his lips and jaw set in a tense line. Her heart wrenched for him. 'That's so sad. Maybe we can change their attitude one day?'

'Good luck trying,' he said wryly. 'I'd like to be a fly on the wall listening to that conversation.'

'We'll work on them together.' Emma tried to be positive.

'I can smell coffee. And something baking?' Emma said a short time later as she and Mal entered Julie's modern kitchen in suburbia, shaking off the raindrops from their damp clothes.

The sisters hugged warmly although it was only days since their harbour lunch together but Julie's attention was immediately diverted by the tall raven haired stranger in her home.

'You must be Mal.'

'In person,' he grinned and accepted her hug.

Emma felt a tug on the leg of her jeans.

'Mia!' Her face lit up and she scooped her niece up into her arms. 'Hey sweetie. It's been a long time. You remember me?'

The child stuck a finger in her mouth and nodded then wriggled to get down again, toddling happily off to play.

Julie rubbed her hands together. 'I have a batch of muffins about ready to come out of the oven but before I make your coffees, guess what?' She nudged her older sister. 'I peed on a stick this morning!'

Emma gasped. 'You're not!'

Julie couldn't stop nodding. 'I phoned Chris at work. He's in disbelief.'

After more hugs all around, they retired to the sofas where Mia nestled onto Emma's lap and happily dropped blueberry muffin crumbs all over them both as the adults ate and drank. An ecstatic Julie seemed blissfully unaware of the mess, her normal high level of domesticity tempered by the fresh news of her pregnancy. Mal stretched out his long legs, watching and listening to the sisters chat.

Too soon, they braved the rain and chill late morning air again to drive further west to their last stop. Emma's parents, Clive and Alice. She suspected this visit might be sticky and braced herself for reproach. Compliments never came easily to them for any of their children. Which was why Julie had determinedly created a loving home for her own family and, after years of university and his internship, Richard moved away, choosing distance to live in freedom.

It seemed to Emma she was the only sibling who had taken the wrong path and regretted it. But all that was changing now. She flicked a glance at Mal's handsome profile and yet again sent up a silent prayer of thanks that she had been nosy about *Clovelly* where fate decided they would meet.

Her parents expected them but there was no joy upon arrival, even after not seeing their daughter for a year. They hugged without affection. Clive and Alice Hamilton loved and were singularly devoted to each other but could not show similar affections for their children. When Emma proudly introduced Mal, it produced guarded reactions. They were polite enough but Alice immediately asked after Steve.

'He's no longer in my life, Mum. We're divorcing, remember? He's moved to Queensland.'

Pointless to explain the dramas of recent days. Her parents lived in their own small limited suburban world, ignorant and trusting. The visit was tedious.

Her parents were shocked when Emma

told them she was staying in Tingara and had bought a cottage. She thought they might be proud. Show just a smidgen of excitement, drop a small word of congratulation but, no. They remained passive and unmoved.

'Come and visit,' Emma offered brightly, despite their lack of enthusiasm.

An empty invitation since her parents never travelled. Looking back now it seemed out of character for them to have moved from Tingara all those years ago, swapping a tiny country town for the largest city in Australia.

Clive didn't even care to visit his aging mother, Mary. Families were fractured in many ways and for equally as many reasons. Mal admitted the struggles with his own parents, too. Emma heaved out a sigh of frustration and made excuses to leave as soon as possible.

Finally, just before midday, with the rain easing they found their way onto the M31 heading south. Toward home. Emma released a sigh of deep pleasure. She phoned Gran along the way who was delighted to hear of their imminent return. Together.

More drained than she realised from the week's adventures, Emma dozed off and on for much of the trip. Mal just kept driving and the hours dragged. Mid afternoon they stopped at a huge cafeteria bakery in

Goulburn for coffee and a snack then pushed on until dark.

Mal's company was undemanding. There were long stretches of comfortable silence between them and Emma could only reflect on how far their relationship had evolved and progressed in just a few short months. Entirely different to her experience with Steve.

So much had happened to affect and change her. And there would be more ahead. She would meet Mal's son, Daniel. *Clovelly* was up for auction next week and she would move into the blacksmith's cottage.

And then the lights of Albury appeared. They bypassed the city and airport where Will had dropped her days before, Emma blithely unaware back then what lay ahead for her in Sydney. Another half hour saw them heading further south into the mountain foothills and Tingara. Home.

It was dark and cold and they were both ravenous. Mate's barking announced their arrival. He nudged Emma's leg so she knelt down to hug him and fondle his ears. 'Missed me, did you, Mate?'

An apron-clad Gran enveloped them in fragile hugs and, when she asked, they promised her full details in the morning.

'Drop your bags in the spare room then and freshen up while I dish out some hot homemade vegetable soup and crusty bread from the bakery. You'll be happy to know Will has haunted me every day,' she muttered as she trotted off toward the kitchen.

Emma and Mal stared at each other.

'She assumes we'll share a room?' He grinned.

'Gran's more broad minded than others her age.'

They did as instructed, loitered in the bedroom for a long and dangerous kiss, and eventually strolled back to the kitchen.

'Ivy and I have been around at the cottage and discussed the garden. We bought some plants at the nursery and booked them up to you,' she told them.

While everyone hungrily spooned up their soup, Emma said, 'Great. I'm hoping to move in next weekend. Clive sends his love.' He hadn't but her son's neglect was the one time Emma was prepared to lie. 'And Julie is going to make you a great grandmother again.'

She beamed. 'Maybe there'll be more,' she pointedly glanced between them.

Emma was tempted to spill the news that she might have another six year old great grandson, Daniel, in her future, but would wait until she and Mal had made definite plans.

Pretending to misunderstand, Emma said,

'As far as I know my brother Richard is still very much single.'

'I wasn't thinking of Richard.'

'I know you weren't. Back off. No pressure, okay?'

Gran heaved a theatrical sign. 'If I must.'

Soon after, yawns all around signalled bed and they all retired, leaving the dishes in the sink until morning.

When the new day dawned, Emma stretched and snuggled into the warm muscled body beside her. 'Is it going to be this wonderful every day?'

'Promise,' he whispered and proceeded to show her exactly how much.

When they eventually appeared for breakfast, spry indomitable Gran, cosily wrapped in her familiar and favourite blue dressing gown, had the makings of pancakes, porridge and a full cooked breakfast already prepared.

With the jug boiled and toast made, the trio crammed around Gran's tiny kitchen table and set to work indulging themselves in a leisurely feast as Emma and Mal explained all that had happened in Sydney during the week.

Mary simply shrugged and said, 'I told you Greenberg was no good.'

Emma winced. 'Okay, I made a mistake. I've moved on.' She and Mal shared a grin.

'Now I don't want to hear him mentioned again. Eat up,' she told them. 'I want to show you my new home and check on progress with my kitchen renovations.'

She also missed her creative jewellery work and longed to reopen at The Stables. With the planned move into the cottage, life was good, if a little crazy right now.

Emma anxiously watched for Mal's reaction as they parked behind a tradesman's vehicle and stepped from the ute out the front of the cottage. His narrowed gaze swept over it all.

'Better than I imagined. It has character,' Mal admitted, looking fascinated.

Deep down, she hoped the historic property would charm him and weave its magic spell, as it had done with her. It was cosy, it was hers and she loved it.

'Wait until you get inside.' She grabbed his arm and dragged him forward beneath the gate arch and up the front path. 'You'll love all its old features.' She halted and turned to Gran trotting along behind them. 'I can see the work you and Ivy have been doing in the garden.'

'That woman is a slave driver. Will carted everything from the nursery for us. He dug the holes and we planted.'

Emma imagined the effort it must have

taken two elderly ladies and felt humbled. Seeing her embarrassment, Gran laid a hand gently on her arm. 'It was our pleasure and gift to you, my dear. You get back what you give and you've been just wonderful to me this past year. I've absolutely adored having you back in Tingara again and I'm over the moon that you're settling here.'

'I'd do anything for you.' Emma blinked back tears.

'I know, my dear, and this is my way of saying *Thank you*.'

'Who did all the weeding?'

'Ivy. She's better on her knees. I was her helper and did as I was told.'

'Well, I owe you all a roast dinner when my kitchen's done and I move in.'

Mal had moved on ahead through the open front door and headed into the interior gloom toward noise coming from the back of the cottage. Emma and Mary followed.

'Oh my word, dear,' Gran breathed.

In the kitchen, Mal was running his hands over the timber bench tops and white cupboards, with the Aga fully installed and taking pride of place.

'It's done.' Emma gasped in amazement. 'I should go away more often.'

'Beautiful workmanship,' Mal acknowledged.

They all shook hands with the carpenter and his workman who stopped for their visit.

'Guys, thank you so much. This is stunning.' Emma beamed.

She stood before the sink and looked out the window over her rear garden. It would come alive with bulbs and flowers and blossom in spring but even now its green dampness and simple magical view down to the creek was uplifting.

Afterwards, Mal went off to see Will about their project. He dropped Mary off at her flat on the way and Emma to The Stables for the day, agreeing to meet up for dinner later.

That evening, Gran apologised for wanting to stay home. 'You two young things go out and enjoy yourselves.'

So Mal and Emma ate at The Tavern. Then, because she itched to see the cottage again, they drove around to it later. Emma flicked on lights. The workmen had left timber so Mal lit a small open fire in the sitting room.

'Feels like home already,' Emma said as they sat on the carpet on the floor staring into the building flames. 'This brings back memories, huh?' she chuckled, as they snuggled closer in the firelight.

'Does it ever. That was the night I fell in love with you,' Mal confided.

'Me, too. But then I didn't dare to hope. The age thing. And Steve still on the scene.'

'We blitzed it all.'

'We sure did. We're a great team.'

'Can't argue with that.' Mal paused. 'I've been thinking. The building project here will keep me busy once it's underway. If you're agreeable, I'd like to live here and make this our home base.'

Emma squealed. 'Yes!'

'I'll still need to commute to Bendigo,' he cautioned. 'One day a week, maybe a Friday then if Brittany agrees, Daniel and I could return for the weekends. Or every other weekend. See how it goes.'

'Of course. I'm dying to meet him.'

'About that, I really need to get back to Bendigo before Monday. Might run it by my men and see if they're interested in buying me out. Running the business together as a joint enterprise, a co-operative. Each to have an interest and share in it.'

'You'd give all that up and move here?' Emma was stoked at his suggestion and that Mal was already giving their future lives together so much thought. Maybe that was why he'd been so quiet on the six hour drive home last night.

'It's what we need to do. Be together. A long distance relationship will be more difficult and doesn't grab me.'

'Me neither.'

'Ideally I'd prefer if we were married,' he said softly.

Emma nodded and barely felt able to breathe for what she hoped might possibly be about to happen. Her heart pounded and her chest exploded with happiness. 'Ideally.'

'Emma Hamilton, the second your divorce comes through, will you marry me?'

'If you and Daniel will have me, yes. Yes. Absolutely.'

She laughed and cried and they kissed, then they made long slow fabulous love by the fire.

Much later, they returned to Gran's flat to sleep but next morning meant goodbyes. Mal to Bendigo and Emma back to work for the last day of the weekend rush at The Stables. Having been together day and night nearly all week, leave-taking proved hard. Mal held Emma tight and she didn't want to let him go. She breathed in his scent, hoping the memory would last all week.

'See you Friday night with Daniel,' he murmured.

11

For Emma, the week was busy yet dragged. The tradesmen finished at the cottage, tidied up and left, after which she spent hours cleaning and unpacking her few basics of furniture stored everywhere but ready to be placed. She tackled the furniture, hauling bed frames and tables into position. Will helped one day with the heavier pieces. She bought linen, made beds and, at the week's end, stocked the refrigerator and pantry.

At dusk on Friday night, she poured a glass of wine and wandered her transformed cottage, admiring every room, checking everything was just right for her first guests. Then she soaked in her claw foot bath and dressed to wait for Mal and Daniel's arrival.

With a hectic week behind her and anxious over meeting Daniel, Emma paced. Since midday she and Mal had exchanged texts and decided pizza would be perfect for dinner. As much as she loved her new kitchen, Emma was grateful to be given the night off.

She saw headlight beams flash across the front windows, and heard the ute engine and voices before her front door bell jangled.

This was it.

She flung it open to be greeted with a bouquet of heavily scented flowers, a broad smile from her man and was instantly swept up into his arms for a very warm Webster welcome. Emma grew intensely aware of the other little human being beside them.

When they broke apart, Mal said, 'Daniel, this is the very special lady I told you about. Emma.'

'Hi,' he said shyly with a trusting grin.

Emma looked down into another pair of very familiar watercolour blue eyes. With dark wavy hair and that dimpled grin, the boy was a mirror image of his father. In the years to come, she could see he would be a heart breaker, too.

'It's lovely to meet you, Daniel. Come inside both of you and get warm,' she fussed nervously.

Mal showed Daniel his bed in the spare room while Emma phoned through their order for pizza. Understandably, the boy clung close to his father for the first part of the evening. Emma was content to remain in the background and watch the dynamics of father and son together.

Daniel was cute, mischievous and well mannered but then he had an awesome role model in his dad who proved loving but firm.

It was clear they shared a strong bond and seeing them together only emphasised how much Emma had begun to realise she wanted this for Mal and herself. A family.

She had hit thirty already. Who was she kidding? She had long since passed *that* milestone. The clock was ticking. Especially since Mia had sought her out in Sydney and snuggled onto her lap, with Julie being so fertile and now Daniel's appearance in her life. Emma was feeling more than a little warm and maternal toward the idea of children of her own.

When Daniel began rubbing his eyes and yawning, Mal bundled him off to bed with a story, his favourite soft brown bear and the promise of ten minutes playing a game on his father's mobile phone. He settled well in a strange room, strange bed and strange house.

'He's a trooper and chilled little guy. Happy anywhere with anyone,' Mal said proudly later.

The next they heard from the lad was when Emma became aware of someone clambering over them. She opened her eyes to pale light and a small voice whispering, 'Wake up Daddy, its morning.'

Mal groaned. 'Morning, champ.'

Daniel giggled and crept under the doona between them. A restless six year old boy in the cottage meant no sleep-ins. Still in pyjamas and dressing gowns, the Aga warming the kitchen and a fresh fire lit in the sitting room, they ate breakfast together. Emma discovered you could never make too many pancakes for a growing boy's bottomless appetite.

'Where are we going this morning, champ?'

'To see a big house.'

'That's right. *Clovelly*. It belonged to my grandfather and it's going to be sold to another family today.'

They dressed, bundled up against the bitter frosty morning cold and braved the brisk walk to *Clovelly*. Mal's suggestion proved wise, since vehicles of all descriptions were parked up and down the full length of Wattle Gully Road for blocks in either direction.

Many, like them, would have come just to witness the passing of a grand and well known old Victorian homestead from its original owner family, the Websters, onto the next generations. They bumped shoulders with many other fellow locals among the huge crowd, including Gran and Ivy.

'No regrets?' Emma murmured to Mal.

He shook his head. 'None. Just pride in her restoration.'

'She's glorious. Everyone here can see and appreciate that.'

The home, as well as being Mal and Daniel's ancestral place, was also the catalyst for their meeting and Emma would always love it for that reason alone.

The auctioneer arrived, Anne Perry standing smartly beside him, clipboard in hand. He read out the formalities and the auction began. Mal had hoisted Daniel onto his shoulders who watched wide eyed and rapt at the whole proceedings, perhaps sensing the importance of the event.

Bidding started without any stalls and jumped even higher at a lively pace. In the end, two interested parties remained. All other early contenders had long since dropped away.

'The bid is over here with this gentleman,' the auctioneer called, indicating the suited man in front. He glanced to the side of the crowd for any further offer from the competition. The price so far was astonishing so the potential buyers clearly knew the big home's value.

'We have another ten thousand,' Anne said pointing to the side.

The front bidder immediately raised his numbered paddle with a counter offer. This process continued for a few more minutes, the crowd gasping at each new raised bid.

Finally the auctioneer bellowed, 'Going.

Going.' There was a loaded pause. 'Gone.' He slapped his hands together. 'Sold to the gentleman in front. Congratulations, Sir.'

They learned the new owner of *Clovelly* was a tree changer property developer from the city who planned to live in the house and make Tingara his new home. He heard Mal did the renovations, sought him out, introduced himself as Seth Duncan and invited him to consider leading his building restoration team on other historic district properties.

'I hate to see them lost,' the man said. 'There are amazing finds tucked away all over the country. We aim to preserve them and give them new life.' He handed Mal the business card for his company. 'Get in touch young man. I like your work.'

He thumped Mal on the shoulder and left to settle the sale.

From the amazement on Mal's face, Emma knew he was stunned with pride. They slapped a high five and beamed at each other.

'Who's that man, Daddy?' Daniel asked as his father swung him down from his shoulders.

'I think he just might be my new boss!'

'Congratulations, Mr. Restoration Team Manager.'

All three were on a high and hardly felt the cold on the return walk back to the cottage.

A week later after Mal overcame his awe at big Seth Duncan's offer, he gathered the courage to phone him. The meeting was a success and Mal bagged himself a brand new job. His Bendigo employees had taken his proposition on board and agreed to his idea of jointly buying him out of the business.

Somehow, Mate became a permanent fixture at the cottage. Gran quietly confessed he was lovely company but too much to handle on her own since she couldn't walk far any more. The dog romped around the back garden, especially when Daniel came for the weekend, and disappeared along the creek to explore.

One weekend, when Daniel had stayed behind in Bendigo for a mate's birthday party, Emma found herself yet again frowning at one particular bare wall in the cottage earmarked for a special purpose.

'Let's go see if Will is finished our painting yet.'

When they arrived at their friend's homely, if untidy, house, he remarked, 'Perfect timing. It's done, so you can do the honours and unveil it.'

Emma gripped the edge of the sheeting covering his work on an easel and whipped it off.

'I hope you like it,' Will murmured humbly beside them.

Speechless, they admired it. 'Oh Will, it's gorgeous. You've captured the blacksmith's cottage beautifully and in every detail.'

Mal shook his hand. 'Can't thank you enough, mate.'

'Our first home,' Emma sighed.

They celebrated with coffee and Will's famous apple cake. Not only was his old clunker of a car but his ability as a cook well known in town.

'We heard from Anne Perry that Ginny Bates has let out St. Anne's for six months as a house swap,' Emma said.

'Yeah. An English girl apparently.'

'So what's Ginny doing then?'

'Got some high powered marketing job in London. Living in the other woman's house apparently.'

Emma laughed. 'Sounds like *The Holiday* to me.' She received a blank stare from both men. 'It's a soppy romance movie. Chicks get it.'

'Not sure I'd trust my home to a complete stranger,' Will said. 'I hope she's respectable.'

'Knowing Ginny,' Emma said, 'She's probably done a full and thorough background check. You can bet the tenant will be perfect. Seeing as she'll be your neighbour, go and introduce yourself when she arrives and then come and tell us what she's like.'

'Wonder how she'll fit into the community?'

'Time will tell,' Mal said.

The conversation drifted on to other things.

It was an hour later before Emma and Mal returned to their cottage to hang their precious new piece of art work and stood back, arms around each other, to admire it.

★　★　★

Two months later, Emma's divorce finally came through so she and Mal could now make wedding plans. They decided on a simple outdoor ceremony, in spring because their garden would look a picture. That mattered because they wanted to be married under the trees down by the creek.

'I hope our parents come,' Emma said.

'Well, mine will only attend from a sense of obligation. Besides, it would look bad if they didn't.'

'Mine, too. They'll grumble at travelling *anywhere* let alone such a long distance. It will be an ordeal for them. On the other hand, Julie and her tribe will be here with bells on even though she's very pregnant now.

She'll be my maid of honour so we'll figure out something for her in a long soft drapey dress.' Emma turned to Mal. 'What about Alex? Can you find him wherever he is in the world?'

Mal chuckled. 'We email. He's been warned. I'm sure he'll be good to go since he's my best man. What about your brother, Richard?'

'He'll be free. He's only surfing up on the north coast. Besides, it will be a good excuse for him to catch up with his mate, Nick Logan, who lives in town.'

'He the guy with the transport business?'

Emma nodded. 'His wife left him so now he's raising his three sons alone. Oh, I can't wait for everyone to be here. We're so blessed. Let's celebrate?' she suggested, high on excitement.

'How?'

She pulled a devilish grin. 'How about skinny dipping in the creek?'

'You're crazy! It's winter!'

'Oh come on. Where's some of that adventurous Webster spirit like your brother Alex?' she teased. 'People in the arctic plunge through a hole in the ice just for fun. Stony Creek will be nothing compared to that. Besides, Gran told me it's thoroughly invigorating.'

Mal raised his eyebrows at the news. 'Mary?'

Emma nodded. 'Plus,' she began tugging at his clothes, 'I have the perfect idea for warming up afterwards.'

'Good thing it's dark and we don't have close neighbours,' Mal shivered a short time later, tip toeing naked through the back garden. Deciding to get it over with and retreat fast back to the cottage, he plunged into the stream first and gasped. 'It's bloody freezing!'

Emma screamed with laughter and jumped in too. 'Think of the memories we're creating,' she said, her teeth chattering, her lips blue. 'And the stories we'll tell our children.'

'We're having kids?'

'Heaps.'

'Okay. Let's escape this icebox and get started then.'

Emma squealed with delight when his big muscled arms went under her legs and he scooped her up, heaving them out of the creek to streak across the grass both frozen and dripping with water.

She had been right. They soon warmed up and their wonderful future beckoned. Emma sent up a prayer of thanks for every blessing in their lives. For eventually finding her place in life, especially the incredible man who had restored her faith in love, would share that wonderful future and be the father of all their little Websters to come.

She sighed over that last thought. The family she had craved for so long would come true. At last.

We do hope that you have enjoyed reading this large print book.

Did you know that all of our titles are available for purchase?

We publish a wide range of high quality large print books including:
Romances, Mysteries, Classics
General Fiction
Non Fiction and Westerns

Special interest titles available in large print are:
The Little Oxford Dictionary
Music Book
Song Book
Hymn Book
Service Book

Also available from us courtesy of Oxford University Press:
Young Readers' Dictionary
(large print edition)
Young Readers' Thesaurus
(large print edition)

For further information or a free brochure, please contact us at:
Ulverscroft Large Print Books Ltd.,
The Green, Bradgate Road, Anstey,
Leicester, LE7 7FU, England.
Tel: (00 44) **0116 236 4325**
Fax: (00 44) **0116 234 0205**

Other titles published by Ulverscroft:

A GENTLEMAN'S BRIDE

Noelene Jenkinson

Anne is forced by circumstances to marry Arthur, the owner of a neighbouring Devonshire farm, whom she hardly knows. When she learns the terrible truth about her husband, however, she fears for her life and flees to Australia. There she meets James, the wealthy owner of a sheep farm. Having been unlucky in love, he has vowed never to fall for another. But he needs heirs to run the farm, and decides to offer a marriage of convenience to the right woman who answers his advertisement in the local newspaper. Anne may just be that woman — but her blossoming romance is threatened when her past returns to haunt her . . .

THE PRIDE OF THE MORNING

Pamela Kavanagh

1850s England: Emma Trigg has always accepted her grandfather's wish for a union between herself and her cousin Hamilton. Their marriage will ensure a continuation of the equestrian tack-making business on Saddler's Row, satisfy her aunt, and provide Emma with a secure future. But at Chester's Midsummer Fair, a chance encounter with personable horse dealer Josh Brookfield sparks a whole different chain of events. A friendship is severed, long-held secrets come to light, and Emma is drawn down an uncertain path. Can she ever forget the man with laughter in his eyes and the soul of a poet?